"They tell me the mountains are full of vampires." Elizabeth looked over at the dead villagers lying in the snow, then covered her eyes with her hands. **"We have to call the police."**

Josef laughed derisively. He stood at least six inches taller than she. Up close, she was striking, almost like a Renaissance portrait, and it made him want to soften, but he was still too furious. "There are two policemen for this entire territory. One of them is an alcoholic, and the other is in league with the vampires."

She shook her head. "I have to know what happened here. It can't be...it can't be what you say it is." She said that now, Josef thought, but she had no idea what the undead were truly capable of.

He heard a branch snap in the nearby woods. "Come on." He half dragged her. He started back down the treeline, sensing something behind them. "Faster," he urged. He wanted to curse her. She was so foolhardy, but she was equally intriguing. Not every woman would travel across the globe to find a missing sibling. Let alone to so remote an area....

ERICA ORLOFF

is the author of *Do They Wear High Heels in Heaven?*, *Spanish Disco* and other titles for Red Dress Ink. She has written for the Silhouette Bombshell line and writes darker fiction for MIRA, including *The Roofer* and *Invisible Girl*. Erica lives in Virginia, where she cherishes the view of the trees and a creek from her office. In her free time, she enjoys her pets, family and friends, and adding to her collection of Buddha statues. Visit her at www.ericaorloff.com, where she regularly blogs about writing. This is her first Nocturne book.

BLOOD SON

ERICA ORLOFF

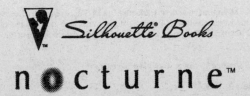

Silhouette Books

nocturne™

 SILHOUETTE BOOKS

ISBN-13: 978-0-373-61756-2
ISBN-10:   0-373-61756-9

BLOOD SON

Copyright © 2007 by Erica Orloff

This edition published by arrangement with Harlequin Books S.A.

® and TM are trademarks of Harlequin Books S.A., used under license.
Trademarks indicated with ® are registered in the United States Patent
and Trademark Office, the Canadian Trade Marks Office and in other
countries.

Visit Silhouette Books at www.eHarlequin.com

Printed in U.S.A.

Acknowledgments

First off, thank you to Margaret Marbury, my ever-wonderful editor, for suggesting that I write another paranormal. I love the new Nocturne line, love writing paranormals, and this has been a wonderful, freeing writing experience.

Thank you to Tara Gavin. From our first conversation, I definitely "clicked" with your vision for this book, and your suggestions have only served to make the story of Josef and Elizabeth more passionate.

Thanks, as always, to my agent Jay Poynor. And to J.D., for seeing me through a stressful couple of months during the writing of this as I tried to complete the manuscript and move up the Eastern seaboard.

Finally, the usual suspects. My friends and family who are always there for me.

To my best friend,
Pam Morrell

Prologue

London, 1972

She usually woke him by humming a lullaby while running her fingers through his curly hair, wrapping dark tendrils around her pinky. Then she'd dress him and take him to work with her, as she kept house for an old gentleman in a stately brick town home near Hyde Park.

But today, she bolted upright in the double bed

in the room they shared, grabbed him fiercely from the cramped crib where he slept, and yanked him to the cold floor. The room was still pitch black. It wasn't yet morning.

"Josef," she whispered frantically, "you must hide."

He rubbed his eyes, clutching at the stuffed polar bear she had given him for his third birthday just the week before.

"Josef." Her voice was desperate sounding. "Whatever happens, do not come out. No matter what you hear. Cover your eyes. Do not come out. Do not make any noise. Do you understand me?"

He nodded, not really comprehending anything but her emotions: fear, terror, grief.

She pulled him to her chest and kissed his cheeks, then rubbed her own cheek against his curly hair. "My baby…" She choked off a sob, but then the tenderness was replaced by a roughness as she pushed him along the floor to the wooden trunk at the foot of her bed. She opened the heavy lid and lifted him inside, moving the spare blankets to make room, then covered him with a scratchy wool afghan. Before she closed the lid, she pushed the blanket aside so he could see her put her finger to her lips, her face pale, sweating.

"Shh, no matter what, darling, no matter what." Then, she pulled the afghan over his head. The lid closed. He was left in complete darkness.

Shivering with fright, he wrapped his small arms around his knees, lowering his head until he was a tightly wound ball. He squinted his eyes shut tight.

At first, all he could hear was his own breathing. His heart. Pounding like a rabbit's. Then, he heard a window breaking, then some hissing, loud, yet guttural. Almost…he would struggle years later to find the word…moist.

Then the keening. Was it them? Her? No, it came from them, a succession of shrieks.

And then her. The nearly inhuman screams of a woman being tortured. She offered up a desperate prayer to God, to be spared. *Please. Help me. Please. Lord.* Eventually, the screams wound down to a plaintive wail. *Just kill me. If you ever loved me, just kill me, Lord.*

Then Josef heard nothing but animal-like slurps

and the gleeful laughter of the insane. Footsteps. Heavy on the floor. The trunk lid lifted, but still he kept his eyes shut.

And then, blessedly, finally, he heard the mechanical screech of sirens.

The trunk lid shut.

Josef listened. He heard scurrying. Like large rats.

Josef waited, eyes still squeezed tight. He was cold, though the trunk was stifling and smelled of moth balls.

The trunk lid lifted again. "In here. It's the little boy!"

Josef felt strong arms pull him out. "I'm a police detective. Don't open your eyes, child," a man's voice whispered. A kind voice. The man smelled of cologne. But mixed with it, all around them, the coppery scent of blood.

He felt the detective's shoulders shake slightly. Josef wrapped his arms tightly around the man's neck, his little fists grabbing at the man's hair. The room was filling with officers. He could hear their deep voices. Could hear Mrs. Burroughs from across the hall, her Irish brogue. "His name is Josef, poor child. Oh, blessed Jesus…Mary, Mother of God, have mercy on her soul."

"Bloody 'ell," one of the officers said. Josef heard a man retching in dry heaves.

Then silence, respectful. Whispering. Josef sensed the sea of humanity filling the room was parting, allowing the detective to carry him out.

Josef started crying. He knew it was bad. *Very* bad.

"Don't look," the detective whispered again, his voice thick.

Josef's eyes hurt from squeezing them so tight. He lifted his head from the detective's shoulder, and then he opened his right eye just a fraction. Then both eyes shot open wide in shock and horror.

The small room was drenched in blood, spatter on every wall. And there she was. His mother.

What was left of her.

And for the rest of his life, Josef regretted opening his eyes. Because after a time, it was the only way he could recall her.

Except in his dreams.

Chapter 1

Prague, present day.

"Please…have you seen the person in this picture?" Elizabeth Martin slid a four by five color photograph of her twin brother, David, across the small round table toward the man sipping coffee at dusk. He didn't understand English, and Elizabeth didn't speak Czech, so she pointed at the photo of David, his smile clearly bright enough to captivate a room, then pantomimed looking around for him.

The coffee drinker gazed down carefully at the photo and shook his head, giving her a shrug, then resumed staring at his laptop.

Elizabeth sighed, scanning the crowded Internet café near the Charles Bridge. This was where David had sent the e-mail from. But Prague was a cosmopolitan city full of people from all over the globe, including the Czech Republic's nearest neighbors— Austria, Germany, Slovakia and Poland. Around her, tongues spoke in so many different languages and dialects, she felt utterly isolated. And then her ears picked up a male voice speaking English. Whipping her head around, she spied a young man with a backpack, scruffy reddish beard, and a tweed newsboy cap, talking with a backpacking counterpart in a thick black fisherman's sweater and sporting a black knit cap. She walked over to them.

"I'm sorry to bother you." She smiled at them. "You speak English?"

They both nodded. "With a brogue, lass," the one with the knit cap said, clear blue eyes dancing.

"I'm looking for my brother. He passed through here maybe two weeks ago, I think. He sent me an e-mail from this café. Do you recognize him?" Elizabeth passed them the photograph.

"David," the one with the red beard said. "Sweet Jesus, what troubles has he gotten himself into? My name's Finn." He stuck out a hand to her. "Sit down."

"Elizabeth Martin," she said, shaking his hand, then gratefully sinking into the wooden chair. "You have no idea how worried I am. When did you last see him?"

He stroked his beard. "About three weeks ago. Right, Tom?" He glanced at his traveling companion, who nodded. "He wasn't himself. Looked fookin'— pardon the language—tired. I was worried he'd picked up something. Flu...something."

"Picked up something?" She tucked a stray black hair behind her ear and gazed down at David's photo. They were so clearly siblings—same shade of black hair, same blue-gray eyes, same pale skin with a rosy tinge around the cheekbones, same cupid's bow forming full lips. She had the faintest smattering of freckles across her nose, and wore her hair nearly to her waist. David kept his shorn close to the scalp, and he wore a simple gold hoop in his left ear. He also had a tattoo, a yin and yang symbol, on his left biceps. In profile, though, they were almost identical, with straight noses and strong, graceful jawlines.

"He looked shaky. He'd been backpacking way the 'ell out past the Liberac region. Past the ski resorts. He was in the Karkonosze. It's January, love. You just don't do that alone and outside the resorts. Too cold to be out there for days on end. I didn't understand it. I mean, go off into the mountains and not ski? Just to be alone?"

She nodded. "That would be David. Always defying conventional wisdom." She paused and bit her lip. "I have to ask you something." She sighed. "Did he seem like maybe he was on…drugs?" She held her breath waiting for the answer. It wouldn't be the first time David had troubles with addiction.

"Could be. Don't know. He was just pale. Thin. Never said anything about drugs, though. We'd even shared a room in a hostel one night just before Christmas. I didn't see anything that made me think he was on something. We each had a pint of ale. That was it."

"Thank you. Any bit of news helps."

"He was heading back there, you know. I don't

get the allure of the isolation, but maybe that's what he wanted," Finn offered. "Maybe he was trying to find himself or something."

"I think that's part of it." Elizabeth nodded.

"Is he in trouble?" Tom asked her.

"I honestly don't know. But thank you." She gave him a feeble smile. "At least I know for sure he was here. And he was in the mountains. I'm trying to trace his route."

"I wish we could tell you more."

"I'm just grateful I even found someone who's seen him. His e-mail...he didn't sound like himself."

Elizabeth stood. "You don't happen to know where he was staying out there, do you?"

"No," Finn said. "But there's an inn out where he said he was. Into the Karkonosze mountains—near the Polish border. The Hawthorn Inn is the English translation of the name. One of the few places in the heart of the mountains where he was hiking and climbing. If he was in those mountains, chances are he either stayed at that inn or passed through. Or someone staying there may have seen him."

Elizabeth nodded.

"Hire a car and driver," Tom said. "Don't go out there alone." He looked over at Finn. "We could travel with you. We're not tied to any schedule. We're just bummin' our way through Europe avoidin' growin' up." He smiled at her.

"Sounds familiar," Elizabeth mused, smiling back. "That's all right. But I'll hire a driver for sure." Elizabeth thanked them both again, shook their hands, and exited the café to go back to her hotel overlooking the Charles Bridge. She walked across the bridge with hundreds of tourists. Built in the 13th century, the Charles Bridge was considered one of Europe's most romantic spots. Each dawn and twilight, tourists strolled across, taking in the view of the red roofs of Prague, or the huge green cupola of the Church of St. Nicholas. Spires rose above the picturesque city, and she felt a pang at how utterly alone she felt. As she walked, she pulled the e-mail out of her purse and unfolded it for the thousandth time since she received it at the University of Virginia, where she taught comparative religion.

Lizzie…

In big trouble. Please. Need help. Someone is trying to destroy me. He even knows what I think before I think it. Come for me. It isn't madness. It is evil.

As Ever,

David

Elizabeth fingered the paper like a talisman, her last communication with him. When it had arrived, she'd gone pale and shut her office door, hands trembling as she waited for her printer to spit the hard copy out. She had easily re-read it a hundred times that night alone.

She had first tried his cell phone. They rarely went a week without talking, using each other as true confidants. For a day or two, his phone would ring once and go to voicemail. After that, she got a message that stated it was a nonworking number. With no further word, she was left to her own imagination.

He even knows what I think before I think it.

She first thought of the possibility of a religious

cult. Certainly, in her studies, she was aware of the world's major religions, but also the thousands of splinter sects. But she couldn't imagine David falling prey to some charismatic cultist. They were both too academic.

Their mother had died in a car accident when they were small—so young they had scant remembrance of her. Their father committed suicide seventeen years later, finally succumbing to the madness that had always choked off his brilliance. He had been an itinerant professor, teaching mathematics at whatever university willing to deal with his bouts of mania in return for his remarkable ability to solve complex proofs, to see the world of formulas in three and four dimensions. After his death—the twins were both juniors in college—she and David had clung to each other and to their studies. She was a Harvard graduate, later a Rhodes scholar; David had attended Harvard as well, studying English with dreams of being a writer. They traveled in the same circles on campus, spent vacations together, bonded as twins, but also by the familial tragedies that affected them both profoundly.

Whereas Elizabeth had pursued academia, getting her doctorate by age twenty-seven, David lost his way, dabbling in drugs, traveling, living off the trust from their parents' estate. But no matter where David was or what he was doing, his tie to her was firm, and she couldn't believe he'd gotten involved in a cult.

Her next thought was drugs. But he'd stopped that years ago. She wondered if perhaps he'd traveled to Amsterdam, maybe fallen in with the wrong crowd. But even that was a stretch. He'd taken to writing more, his old ways behind him. At their thirtieth birthday five months ago, spent touring the National Gallery in D.C., he had seemed grounded to her.

Which left the one thought she didn't want to face. Madness. He'd never exhibited signs of it before. They both watched each other closely, like all children of the insane, wondering if a crying jag, a bout of depression, a stretch of insomnia was a sign the illness had come for them, too. But it hadn't…until now, perhaps.

Elizabeth's mind wandered and fretted until she reached her hotel. She spoke to the concierge in the lobby and arranged for a car and driver for the following day.

Tired, worried, stressed, she ordered a simple but heavy Czech meal of liver dumpling soup—Elizabeth had discovered Czechs loved dumplings—a hearty dark rye bread coated in sesame seeds and a glass of robust red wine sent to her room, and then went up to change. Room service arrived and set the tray on her table. She ate quietly, reading a book by St. Thomas Aquinas, trying not to let her mind wander to her worries. Eventually, though, she gave up, after reading the same paragraph over and over, unable to retain a single thought. She put on her nightgown, and gazed out on the now-dark city. It was breathtakingly beautiful, glowing with light and yet retaining its Old World elegance.

Despite David's disappearance and strange missive consuming her thoughts, she felt a melancholy longing for companionship. She dated, she'd been proposed to twice—and turned both men down, though the break-ups had been amiable. But she was certain she had never been in love. She wondered if her I.Q. kept up her emotional guard, isolated her.

Or was it fear of the kind of passionate love so akin to her father's mania? Mad love. Whatever the reason she avoided it in the past, she found herself wishing for a connection to someone now, halfway across the globe and vulnerable.

She remembered a few times, trying to explain her father to boyfriends. Her father was so brilliant that being around him was intoxicating. He not only loved mathematics, but also quantum physics from the tiniest protons to the big bang. He ran family dinners almost like a salon. She and David and he would debate the existence of God, the birth of the universe, the string theory and existentialism. As young teens, they learned to defend their views; their opinions were valued and respected as long as they could articulate a defense. But the other side of their genius dad was his dark days. She and David tried to rally around him, tried to get him to see beyond the suffocating depression, the madness closing in on him, but the paranoia and anger and rage were too overpowering. No one understood how she could adore him yet fear him. Only David knew how shining the good times were.

She longed, she supposed, to find a soul mate. Someone who could challenge her mind and soul like those shining times, like their dinning room table salon. She wondered, as her years went on, single and alone, if she wished for too much.

Elizabeth withdrew from the window and turned down her comforter, feeling the effects of jet lag, and climbed into bed. She said her prayers, crossing herself out of habit. She and David were lapsed Catholics. After their father's death, their faith foundered. But old habits died hard, and she always said her prayers each night, certain in the vastness of the universe, from the smallest proton to infinity, in something. Someone.

She fell asleep rapidly, as if a black velvet curtain was drawn across her mind. Soon, she was dreaming. She was running through the woods, being chased by unseen attackers. Brambles cut her cheeks, tore her clothes, tugged at her hair. She fought to escape the forest's beasts. She heard hissing, voices, eerily inhuman. She sensed David, there and yet unreachable. Sometime in the night, Elizabeth gasped and bolted upright in bed, clawing at her throat, unable to breathe.

She coughed, and finally her lungs filled with

precious oxygen. She touched her forehead and knew she had a fever. She was drenched in sweat. And she still felt breathless.

Elizabeth knew that Prague was infamous for its pollution problems in winter, the smog trapped by cloud cover, mountains and cold. She assumed that was what was causing her to gasp.

She turned on her bedside lamp, and climbed out of bed to go get a glass of water. She turned on the bathroom light squinting as the brightness bounced off of the ultra-modern white tiles. And then she saw them.

Leaning in close to the mirror she stared in terror at her neck. Two tiny red marks were raw and bleeding. She moved her hand to her throat to wipe at the droplets of blood, and they disappeared. She had imagined them. Trembling, she turned on the faucet and splashed cool water on her face, trying to force the nightmare away.

And not for the first time, Elizabeth Martin wondered if she and David were destined to repeat their father's fall from the pinnacles of academia.

Had David lost his mind?

And was she following in his footsteps?

Chapter 2

By morning, Elizabeth had shrugged off the hallucination as a lingering nightmare. She checked out of her room, and brought her suitcase to the lobby where she met her chauffeur. Dima was a charming Russian with a closely shaved head that she could tell disguised encroaching baldness. He looked about fifty or so, and deep crags settled in by his soulful brown eyes. He bowed deeply upon meeting her, then winked playfully before loading her suitcase in the trunk of his black Mercedes sedan while she reviewed her final bill and settled her account.

She told him she wanted to travel deep into the mountains near the Polish border, heading to a small inn nestled in the Karkonosze. Settling into the backseat, she looked out the window as they drove through Prague then got onto a highway and headed northeast, a view of mountains and wintry landscape as far as her eyes could see.

"You don't have skis," Dima remarked once he had maneuvered them onto open road. He gunned the engine, and she could see the speedometer climb.

"No. I don't ski. Not well, that is," she said, smiling at the memory of falling down the bunny hill while learning with David when they vacationed in Vermont together with their father one year.

"It's very…isolated, the place you're going. I know where it is on the map. It's not like Prague. She's a beautiful city, no?"

"Prague is lovely. I hope to come back to it someday. But I'm looking for my brother. He's missing. Sort of. I'm not even really sure, but the last place he was seen…was the mountains."

"A skier?"

"No. I think he was backpacking."

"You better be careful."

"I will. I'm used to traveling. I studied in London, and lived for a year with my father and brother in Cambridge as a child."

"No, I mean the people there are not used to strangers. They're superstitious. Go, find your brother, and then leave. A beautiful woman like you should be in the city, with its art and its people."

Elizabeth saw him look at her in the rearview mirror, his brows knit together.

"I'll be careful, I promise." She was bemused by his mother-hennish worry layered with flirtation.

"Don't go out alone at night."

"I won't." Elizabeth tried to hide a smile. She couldn't decide if Dima was flirting with her outright or being paternal.

"There's tales up there. Wild things come out at night."

"Well, I promise to remain in my room with the door locked." She caught his eye in the mirror and did a gesture of "cross my heart."

"Good." He nodded.

Elizabeth leaned her head back against the leather seat and shut her eyes. She thought back to the night when she urged David to go to rehab. It was the summer after their senior year. He had their father's brilliance. As long as he attended a lecture, his photographic memory enabled him to take the exam and ace it without studying. Even attending lectures nursing a wicked hangover qualified. And he certainly attended his fair share with bruising hangovers.

At first, she wasn't worried. She figured his partying had to do with sowing his wild oats. That she *hadn't* felt the need to sow them didn't bother her. That was David, the life of the party.

But then it got more complicated. She visited his dorm as graduation approached and found him passed out so deeply, she couldn't rouse him. Frightened, she had rifled through his drawers, certain he was on something harder than alcohol—and she had been right when she found handfuls of pills.

She and his roommate got him up—and after he came down from his high, after a few cups of coffee and a long night of talking, the story of his reliance on pills came out. It was, he told her, his way of making the pain of their combined losses go away. He floated to somewhere else, to those gleaming happy moments when their father wasn't ill.

Elizabeth sighed at the memory. David was the one people gravitated to, sparkle and charm, and yet he was the more fragile one. She was, in the words of his psychologist at his rehab center, the responsible one. And wasn't it so? She had always made sure dinner was on the table, even when their father was so wrapped up in a new proof that he forgot to eat for hours and even whole days on end. She made sure their shirts were pressed, their laundry done. David helped. He made his bed each day and did his homework each night. He brewed the coffee the way their father liked it—and prepared Papa's scotch the way he liked it, too. But it was Elizabeth who bore the weight of it all, right down to planning the funeral because David couldn't bear it.

She shook her head at the memories. The Mercedes' ride was so smooth, she felt cradled

against the leather seats. She tried to recall something happy. Something wonderful to focus on. That
was easy. David had come to visit her in Charlottesville the year before, and they decided to take
a long hike into the Blue Ridge. They talked the
whole time, and as they descended the mountain
trail in the very late afternoon, they saw a spectacu-
lar sunset, as if the mountains were bursting with
flames of glory. David whispered, "It's like a chuch,
you know?" And she had understood, as she always
understood David, and quoted John Fowles, one of
her favorite writers: "In some mysterious way woods
have never seemed to me to be static things. In
physical terms, I move through them; yet in meta-
physical ones, they seem to move through me."
David had clasped her hand, and they stood until the
last orange embers faded between two mountains
and then descended the rest of the path to their car,
driving home in companionable silence.

At the memory, after the previous night's restless
sleep, Elizabeth soon nodded off and didn't awaken
until they were nearly at the Hawthorn Inn several
hours later. She roused and rubbed her eyes, looking
out at thick forests of firs and tall mountains that

loomed above her, blocking out the sun and giving the sky a gloomy texture.

Dima pulled off the narrow mountain road, which had no guardrails and made Elizabeth nervous, down a side road that wasn't even paved—a gravel- and dirt-packed pathway to the inn.

"I don't like the look of this place," Dima said protectively.

"It will be fine," Elizabeth assured him as he pulled past the inn's stone and wrought-iron gates and parked. She climbed out of the car. The inn was a two-story gray stone structure that looked more fortress rising in the mist than cozy bed and break-fast. It had a slate roof, and gargoyles perched on pillars near the eaves, keeping silent watch.

"It almost looks like it used to be a monastery, don't you think?" she asked Dima, pointing up at one gargoyle with a grotesque protruding tongue.

He nodded and crossed himself. Then he popped the trunk open and took out her suitcase. As they got close to the door, he whispered, "You have my card. If you want to return to Prague call me, and I will come get you. Right away."

"Thanks," she said softly back. She rang the doorbell and after a moment or two, the immense wooden door swung open.

"Hello." Elizabeth smiled.

"Yes?" The woman who answered the door was short and stocky, wearing a simple housecoat, washed until it was threadbare in spots. Her wiry gray hair was tucked into a plain blue-and-white-checked scarf and she carried a homemade-looking broom of real straw. Her skin was remarkably unlined, though her face was jowly. Elizabeth guessed the woman was maybe in her late sixties—her hands were quite wrinkled, Elizabeth presumed both from age and from cleaning an inn this size, day in and day out.

"I'm looking for a room for the night."

"For both of you?" the woman answered in thickly accented English as she eyed Dima suspiciously.

"No, just me."

The woman put a hand on her ample hip and nodded. "Okay. Come in."

Elizabeth and Dima followed her. Then Elizabeth bid him good-bye with a hug.

"Remember what I said," he warned her. "Stay in at night. Doors locked."

Elizabeth nodded and watched him leave, listening to the sound of his tires on the gravel as he drove away. Then Elizabeth and the woman proceeded to an enormous wooden desk. In the center was a thick leather book, opened to a page of signatures. The woman told her to sign the register. Elizabeth's heartbeat quickened when she saw David's name next to a date about three weeks prior.

"This name here." She pointed at his familiar scrawl—he was left-handed, as was she, but he had always written in narrow chicken-scratch style, virtually illegible. "Do you recall him?"

The woman looked at David's name, blanched, then shook her head. "No."

"But you haven't had that many guests out here since." She counted the names on the register. "You would remember him. He's tall. Black hair. Pale eyes. Thin. Dimple over here." Elizabeth pointed at her cheek. "Looks very much like me."

"No." The woman was stone-faced. She had set

the broom against the wall, and now she crossed her arms in front of her chest.

Elizabeth sighed. "Well, then there must be other people who work here."

"Just my husband. I am Anna. He's Zoltan."

"Perhaps I could speak with him."

"He's not here right now. Later. Maybe."

Sensing she was getting nowhere, and yet certain there was a reason the innkeeper denied seeing David, Elizabeth merely nodded. "Fine. Can you show me to my room, then?"

The woman eyed Elizabeth warily, then took an intricate brass key from a row of hooks. "Come."

Elizabeth hefted her own suitcase and followed behind Anna as she ascended the large main staircase, with its ornate banister.

Looking to forge a friendlier connection, Elizabeth offered, "The inn is beautiful. The architecture…the windows." As they reached the top of the landing, Elizabeth spied a stained glass window of a bushy tree with pointed thorns. "Ah, so this is why it's called the Hawthorn Inn."

The woman nodded, looking up. "This used to be a convent."

"Really? How fascinating."

The woman turned to look at Elizabeth. "This is sacred ground."

"Well, the window is beautiful." Elizabeth followed the old woman down a long, dim hallway, the heels of her boots clicking and echoing behind the woman's shuffling gait. At the very end, the woman unlocked a door, and opened it. "Supper is at eight. Promptly."

Elizabeth put her suitcase down and was going to ask a question, but when she turned around, Anna was already gone.

Elizabeth scanned her room. It was as bare and austere as she supposed an actual convent might be, with a large pewter crucifix hanging right above the headboard of the double bed. The crucifix was of a particularly agonized Christ, his face contorted into such an expression of pain, Elizabeth felt the need to look away, as if it were too personal.

The rest of the room was plain. Stone floor, without a single mat or rug to soften it, a wooden chair with a straight, high back. Simple white sheets and chenille spread on the bed. One dresser made of a dark wood. A small coal stove for heat, with a black metal bucket of coal next to it and a hand shovel. No phone. No television. Not even a clock radio. Elizabeth spied a single kerosene lantern and some candles. Looking around, she saw no outlets. The room didn't have power.

The lone, large window was arched, like a church's, and the panes of glass were frosted. Elizabeth unlocked the window and pushed out, a rush of frigid air hitting her face and making her cheeks tingle. Her room overlooked a field leading back to a small cottage surrounded by hawthorn bushes. Beyond that, she saw the mountains, rising so high their peaks were concealed by clouds.

Elizabeth closed the window so as to keep out the chill and started to unpack. Technically, she could stay in the Czech Republic until the middle of January, when she had to return for classes. She had spoken to her department chair, a former lover and dear friend named Martin Green. He had assured her that she could have as long as she needed, even if he had to teach her classes for a week or two himself.

She had about ten days' worth of clothes, mostly jeans and thick sweaters and turtlenecks, with a single black cocktail dress and shoes and two elegant shawls. She hung the dress, put the rest in the bureau, and decided to stroll the grounds until dinnertime.

She descended the large staircase again, her gaze once more transfixed by the intricate stained glass hawthorn bush with its dangerous thorns. As a religious scholar, she knew that the hawthorn was sometimes considered a sacred bush, its thorns reminiscent of the thorny crown of Christ. In medieval times, small crowns of hawthorn were often hung above infants' cradles to keep them safe.

Elizabeth didn't see the innkeepers downstairs, so she pushed out on the wooden door and wandered outside, finding a path in the woods. Her boots crunched on fairly fresh snow, and the air was crisp and not polluted as near Prague. She inhaled deeply, feeling the clear air lift her spirits a bit. A cloud cover of fogginess clung to the ground. She spied a trail up a nearby hill and climbed it, feeling a little breathless, she supposed from the altitude. At the top, she tried to survey the landscape, but the fog doomed her efforts. However, she was very sure that the inn was nestled in between mountains, keeping it isolated. She wondered who ever frequented the place and whether there was a nearby village. She imagined that an avalanche in the mountains would not bode well for the inn, which was at the very foot of one of the tallest peaks.

She continued walking, trying to release some of the stress she felt over David. At home in Charlottesville, she lived in a small cottage-style home nestled near the Blue Ridge Mountains. She loved to hike and horseback ride, and being outside in nature always de-stressed her—as well as David. Their vacations had always centered around trips to majestic natural wonders, like the cruise they once took through Alaska.

She walked, allowing her worries to leave her temporarily. The sun set rapidly, and she was virtually unaware of it until the day's gloom increased with the coming of night. She started down the hill, when a man came charging up the incline toward her, a furious expression on his face.

"You crazy American, come on. Get inside!" He

grabbed her roughly by the arm, and she could feel his strong fingers digging into her.

"Excuse me." Elizabeth took the man for about sixty, stocky with gray bushy eyebrows. She guessed him for Anna's husband, Zoltan.

"You must get inside. Hurry!"

Nearly tripping as he pulled her down the hill, Elizabeth tried to chalk up his attitude as Old World chauvinism, but her chauffeur's words lingered in her head. Maybe it was superstition and folklore at work.

Jerking her along by her upper arm until it hurt, they made it back to the inn as Elizabeth heard a kind of howling or keening in the woods.

"What was that?"

"Wolves. Come."

He half-pushed her through the front door, locking it behind him with a bolt and then a large brass key.

"You cannot go out after dark. The wolves come."

"All right," she replied, feeling slightly unnerved by the thought that she was essentially a prisoner until morning. "If you had only told me, I wouldn't have gone off alone. You frightened me, pulling me back here like that."

He seemed to ponder this. "Okay. I'm Zoltan."

"Elizabeth Martin." She put out her hand, and he shook it, then gave her a little smile, perhaps declaring a truce.

"I'm sorry to scare you."

"It's okay." She softened.

He sighed, started to say something, then seemed to think the better of it. Yet, a moment or two later, he blurted out, "You are the American's sister."

Elizabeth felt a surge of hope. "You remember him?"

Zoltan nodded. "Come. We eat. Drink. I tell you."

Elizabeth followed him down a dark hallway on the main floor. Occasional sconces held thick candles. Elizabeth felt an unfamiliar nervousness, finding herself dashing from one circle of flickering light to the next, hurrying behind Zoltan, and rushing even more in the darkened sections of corridor. Finally they reached the dining room. It contained one long oak table that could easily seat thirty. Candles were set on it in heavy pewter candelabras, along with three heavy glazed ceramic plates, lead crystal wineglasses, pewter utensils and a bottle of red wine. Anna came out of the adjoining kitchen balancing a tray.

"Dumplings. Potatoes. Dark bread. Butter. Good?"

Elizabeth nodded. "I hadn't realized how hungry I was. But now that I smell your cooking, I'm famished."

Anna, dour earlier when Elizabeth first arrived at the inn, brightened at the compliment. She set the tray down then slapped Zoltan on the arm. "See. I tell you she like it."

He nodded and said playfully, "You are always right, Anna. I must learn after forty years. Always right." He winked at Elizabeth.

At that, Anna smacked his arm again. "Wise guy."

The three of them sat down, and Zoltan made a motion for Elizabeth to bow her head. He said grace in what she assumed was Czech, and then he crossed himself. Anna did the same, then so did Elizabeth.

"Now we eat," he proclaimed.

Anna put heaping ladles of doughy dumplings and potatoes on her dish.

Elizabeth tasted a forkful. "So tender. This is wonderful!" She ate hungrily and tried to be patient, waiting for Zoltan to tell her about David. She sensed if she pressed them, the married couple would turn silent again. Red wine was freely poured. A second bottle came out. Then Zoltan had seconds, and finally, he leaned back, patted his stomach in a gesture of fullness, and said, "He was here. Your brother."

Anna nodded, not looking at Elizabeth, perhaps feeling guilty for lying earlier that day.

Elizabeth leaned her elbows on the table. "Was he all right?"

The innkeepers exchanged glances. Then Zoltan said softly, "I do not think so."

Elizabeth bit her lip. "Please tell me."

He placed both hands on the table. "This…" He knocked on the wood. "This is where the good sisters ate. Upstairs—" he pointed at the ceiling "—is where they slept. It is holy ground. They first came here well over a century ago to help the isolated villages out here. They made bread, and they kept honeybees. They kept a large garden. And they wove cloth. They all kept a vow of silence, however."

"When did you take it over?"

"When all the sisters left," whispered Anna.

"You see," Zoltan said. "One by one, they died of old age. And the ones that remained, over time…they believed the villagers who said there were vampires here."

He paused, seemingly waiting for Elizabeth to react. She blinked hard. "Vampires?" As a religious scholar, she was used to superstition.

"Yes." He said it resolutely. "We have heard them. Seen their handiwork."

"And the sisters believed in them?" Elizabeth found it hard to comprehend that Catholic nuns would believe in mythical creatures. It would be against all doctrine.

"Yes. That is why the hawthorn trees. To kill vampires. Arrows and stakes, and even crosses made of them. The stained glass. All to keep the vampires away. But the sisters were prisoners here. Sacred ground kept them safe, but one winter…the vampires cut off their food supply. The sisters used to take delivery of flour and staples before the heavy snows. When the villager who brought the supplies was murdered in cold blood, the supplies destroyed, they were left to starve."

"Couldn't they get word out?" Elizabeth asked. Not that she believed in vampires, but certainly she could believe their supplies were somehow waylaid.

"When the Mother Superior left to get help, she was murdered. Two sisters starved to death or died of old age that winter. We found their journals. When spring arrived, a priest came to shut it down. The remaining sisters were eventually sent to other convents, and this place was abandoned. Until we came along. We have restored it. We…were born in the mountains. We won't let the vampires drive us away."

"And how do you know there are vampires?" Elizabeth asked, trying to be respectful of the cultural beliefs of the older couple.

"We have seen. Bloody animals in the woods," Anna said.

"Many things," Zoltan said. "Your brother had two marks. Here." He pointed at his neck.

Elizabeth inhaled sharply. Her dream. Her hallucination. She was still bound to David, no matter what had happened to him. He was her twin, her other half. When they were little they had their own language. She thought of the subject line of the e-mail he sent from Prague. *Shakelpe.* Their "language" for help. That way Elizabeth could be certain it was from him.

"So where is he? Why did he leave?"

"The vampires were chasing him, tormenting him. He hadn't slept in weeks. He left by daylight to get back to Prague, but he will have discovered by now he can't simply escape them. They will lure him back here."

"Have you seen him then, since he left?"

"No, but we hear them. On the mountains."

"Hear them?"

"The wolves."

Elizabeth again tried to be respectful. "But how do you know they're not ordinary wolves?"

"Josef can tell you."

"Josef? Who's he?"

"Our dhampir," said Anna, proudly.

Elizabeth struggled to understand. "Your dhampir? Isn't that the child of a mortal mother and a vampire father?"

"Yes." Anna smiled.

"*Your* dhampir. You mean he is here?" Elizabeth

asked incredulously. She assumed they meant a garden statue or something.

Anna nodded. "He is ours. This convent's. He lives in the caretaker's cottage."

"The one with the hawthorn around it?"

Zoltan nodded. "He is very untrusting. He suffers."

"Suffers?"

They both nodded. "We care for him," Anna said. "In return for his protection."

"Will he talk to me?" Elizabeth certainly didn't believe in vampires or dhampirs. But if he could cast some light onto David's whereabouts, she'd talk to the boogeyman for all she cared.

"I do not think so. He knows you're here, though. Maybe, if you can gain his trust," Zoltan offered.

"If we talk to him, perhaps. Right, Zoltan?"

"Perhaps."

"Please do, then," Elizabeth pleaded. "I'll try to see him tomorrow."

"Okay." Zoltan nodded.

Anna stood up. "I have pie. Apple and raisins."

"Oh, can I beg off and have a piece tomorrow? If you don't mind, I think I'm going to go up to bed."

"You rest, dear," Anna said. "The pie will keep if this one—" she jerked her head toward her husband "—doesn't stuff himself. Look at that belly!"

Elizabeth stood, laughing. "Thank you both. And dinner was delicious."

"Good night, Elizabeth," Zoltan said.

Elizabeth left the dining room, her head spinning from red wine and the feeling like she had dropped into the middle of the seventeenth century. Vampires? What next?

She made her way up the staircase to the hawthorn stained glass window. Had the isolation made the good sisters of the convent go mad?

And more importantly, had that madness and isolation gotten to her brother?

Chapter 3

Josef Darecky knelt at the small altar in the corner of his bedroom. On the simple wooden table, covered with a lace cloth, sat a photo of his mother in a silver frame, a beeswax candle he always kept lit—replacing the votive every night—and a plain wooden cross.

"Protect me, Mother," he whispered as he crossed himself, head bowed. He lifted the silver crucifix that hung from a chain around his neck and kissed it.

He stood slowly, painfully. For as long as he could

remember, he had a searing burn in his heart, from the murder of his mother, and a vicious pain throughout his body from the curse of his father. His bones ached, an agony that made some nights nearly unbearable. He had researched what little he could on what he contemptuously called "his condition." In the myth and lore of vampires, bone afflictions were common. But nowhere had he read of anything that was helpful.

Anna tried. Her poultices did bring a little relief. He had traveled to Prague, where one doctor diagnosed him with osteoarthritis, another with fibromylagia, and yet another wanted to test him for lupus. But Josef knew he had none of those. He tried their modern medicines, their opiates and pain relievers. None of them worked.

Pain was his cross to bear. He learned to travel deep within, through meditation and prayer. That was the only relief he had.

He shut his eyes, as he always did before the hunt, and imagined himself free of pain, running up the side of the mountains, every nerve on fire, every sense aware. He pictured himself pulling his arrows out, loading them in his bow, and striking every quarry at which he took aim.

Josef opened his eyes, put on his pack, took his bow from the wall, and exited his cottage, his height causing him to duck his head slightly at the door. He parted the hawthorn bushes and made his way to the mountain.

He heard them first. Far off and distant, but his own senses were nearly as keen as theirs. When he was younger, his adoptive parents used to wrap his eyes in soft bandages at night, and put cotton balls in his ears, just so he could sleep. As he grew older, he had to learn how to shut out the noises himself.

He crept up the side of the mountain in the cold, dressed like a commando in black pants and a black sweater, a black knit cap pulled over his head, black coal smudged on his face. The moon was playing hide and seek behind some clouds, and he started running along the treeline when he heard a shriek.

Josef burst through a clearing, and saw them. Four wolves were circling two bodies lying on the ground, snarling, teeth bared. He was too late. The male victim was already disemboweled, his body torn to shreds. The female victim was lying limp and pale on the fresh snow. She was a villager. He thought he recognized her. The wolves were pacing around her, growling, snapping their jaws in a sickening taunt. When he came into the clearing, as if in unison, they turned toward him.

With swift, well-practiced movements, Josef took an arrow, loaded it into his bow, aimed, and pierced one wolf in the chest. It rose on its two hind legs with a deafening roar, before falling to the snow, its body reverting to its vampire form as ligaments and bones snapped, an arrow in its human-appearing chest, black blood oozing onto the snow.

The other wolves reacted as if in a feeding frenzy. They lapped at the blood. Josef took out another arrow and aimed. This time, he pierced the hindquarters of a shaggy-coated silver wolf. It reacted by howling, but it did not turn back in form—Josef had learned that only happened if he struck the heart.

He plucked another arrow from his pack, now moving so quickly that any of his own pain was forgotten in the surge of adrenaline mixed with fury. He knew the black wolf was their leader, but the black wolf rarely came out with the pack. Instead, Josef learned by tracking them, they often brought back part of their kill to the black wolf deeper still in the forest, so far in Josef usually lost the trail.

He killed a second wolf, then a third, which left only the gray wolf injured in its hindquarters. It circled Josef, limping but fierce, its eyes narrowed, black-hued saliva trailing to the snow. It was strengthened by lapping the blood of the fallen vampires.

Josef pulled another arrow from his pack. Then he heard a high-pitched shriek, a woman's scream. The sound brought him back to the small room he shared with his mother in London and sent a violent jolt through his spine. He turned his head and saw the woman from the inn, the American that Zoltan told him was searching for her brother.

"Fool!" he shouted at her. "Go back to the inn!" His head was turned when the gray wolf leaped on him, sending Josef to the ground, where he landed in the hard-packed snow. Pain reverberated through his body, and he held off the wolf with his forearm.

Josef could hear the woman. She was screaming over and over in hysteria. The wolf lifted its head and growled in her direction, then turned back to Josef, jaws snapping. The beast was so close to Josef's throat that Josef smelled the blood on its breath, and its saliva dripped onto his face.

In the fraction of a moment the wolf was distracted by the American's screams, Josef had pulled his large hunting knife from its sheath. He jammed the razor-sharp blade upward, using all his force to drive it through the wolf's ribs and, with another thrust, penetrated into its chest cavity. When Josef pierced its heart, the wolf began to transform back to its vampire form, human, pale and cold. Dead. Permanently.

Pushing the vampire off of himself, Josef rolled onto his side and took a deep breath, trying to tamp down the pain deeper inside himself where he could control it. Slowly, he rose. Then he remembered the female villager. He scrambled to her side, but she had already taken her last breath, her pupils open and fixed, staring up at the uncaring moon. By morning, it would appear that she and her companion were killed by wild animals, and the vampires would have been turned to ash by the rising sun.

Josef now faced the American woman, furious.

"Why have you followed me? You could have been killed. Your stupidity could have caused me to miss, to have been killed myself."

He stormed through the snow toward her. She was trembling and crying, and he shook her shoulders. "I asked you a question. Why are you following me? Didn't Zoltan warn you not to leave the inn at night? Do you have a death wish?"

She shook her head and took a deep breath. Then she pulled away from him. "No, I don't have a death wish. I heard the howling. I was watching your cottage from my bedroom window. I saw you leave, and I thought..." She hesitated.

"You thought what?" Josef growled. He stood at least six inches taller than she. Up close, she was striking, almost like a Renaissance portrait, and it made him want to soften, but he was still too furious. "You thought what?" he repeated a little more gently.

"I thought maybe I could find out what Zoltan and Anna were so afraid of. What the hawthorn means. They tell me the mountains are full of vampires, but…I…" She looked over at the dead villagers lying in the snow, then covered her eyes with her hands. "We have to call the police."

Josef laughed derisively. "Impossible. There are two policemen for this entire territory. One of them is an alcoholic who makes rotgut potato-vodka moonshine in his bathtub, and the other is in league with the vampires."

The American woman started shivering, Josef guessed from shock and cold. "Come on," he urged her. "We need to get you inside."

She shook her head. "I have to know what happened here. It can't be…it can't be what you say it is. What Zoltan and Anna say it is. It can't."

Josef heard a branch snap in the nearby woods. He didn't like being out in the open, saddled with a hysterical woman. "Come on." He half-dragged her, starting back down the treeline, sensing something behind them. "Faster," he urged. He wanted to curse her. She was so foolhardy, but she was equally intriguing. Not every woman would travel across the globe to find a missing sibling. Let alone travel to so remote an area.

She struggled under his grasp. "We can't leave those bodies there."

"The villagers will find them in the morning, when it is safe."

"But…"

He finally had enough. "Listen, you have no idea what you're up against. If you want to end up like the dead woman up there—" he pointed "—be my guest. Otherwise, we've got to get to the inn. To sacred ground."

She stared up at him. Her eyes, he noticed, were a peculiar gray color, nearly transparent and strangely hypnotic. "Fine," she whispered, and followed along beside him as he rushed down the mountain, branches occasionally scratching their faces. When they got to the inn's grounds, he parted the hawthorn bushes and they stood outside his cottage, his hand still holding tightly to her arm. Maybe a hundred yards off, he heard a wolf's call. One had been tracking them.

"Do you want to come in?" he offered. "I'll start a fire." Maybe he had been too quick to scold her. He could offer her at least what little information he had.

Her eyes were now mistrusting. "No. I'm going

to the main house. I climbed out through a window in the pantry."

"Hurry then," he said and released his grip on her arm. "Off with you."

She turned away toward the inn. Then she stopped in her tracks. "Do you know where my brother is?" she asked, glancing back over her shoulder.

He didn't answer.

"Is he with them? Those things?"

Josef tried to recall how he felt when he first began to understand what his mother suffered. When he was older, when he put all the pieces together.

"Maybe," he said finally.

She turned her back to him, but he noticed she straightened, held her head higher. "I'm *going* to get my brother back," she said. "No one…no *thing,* can stop me."

He watched her until he could no longer see her in the darkness. She said that now, Josef thought, but she had no idea what the undead were truly capable of.

Chapter 4

Elizabeth heard a soft rapping on her door the next morning. She climbed from bed, her feet gingerly stepping on the icy-cold floor. She had barely slept. Every time she shut her eyes, visions of blood spilling on the snow filled her mind. She wondered if it was another dream or hallucination. What was this place?

She opened the door, and Anna stood there with a tray laden with home-baked biscuits and kolaches, and a pot of what smelled like fresh-brewed coffee.

"Oh, Anna… Thank you," Elizabeth said gratefully. Her stomach rumbled with hunger.

"You'll catch the death of a cold with bare feet on these floors. Climb back into bed," Anna clucked. "Go on. You'll have a nice hot breakfast in bed."

"Please don't fuss," Elizabeth urged.

"Nonsense. Go on." Anna nodded.

Elizabeth realized Anna was a formidable opponent unused to anyone disobeying her loving iron rules. She returned to bed and pulled the covers up over her lap.

"Zoltan found the pantry window ledge had been cleared of snow on the outside," Anna remarked as she plopped the tray down on Elizabeth's lap and started pouring coffee. "As if someone had slipped out in the night." She raised an eyebrow.

Elizabeth picked up a kolache and nibbled at a corner. "This is delicious," she said softly, deliberately avoiding the inference.

"We heard the wolves last night. It was dangerous for you to go outside. Please, please stay in. Let Josef take care of the vampires."

Elizabeth shook her head. "Anna...you can't accept this all so easily, can you?"

Anna shrugged. She walked over to the coal-burning stove and placed several coals in it, in an attempt to warm the room. "You think I'm a simple woman from the mountains. Superstitious. Right? You think I am not educated."

"No, Anna. It's not that." Elizabeth frowned, fearing that she had hurt her new friend's feelings. "It's just...I *saw* what they did last night. But I still cannot accept it. Do you understand? It's too insane. It's...not real."

The old woman nodded. "I understand. Maybe for me, it was easier to accept. I lived through World War II. I was a little girl. I saw what mankind can do. I saw cattle cars full of human beings. Is that any more insane or cruel than a vampire?"

Elizabeth was quiet for a moment. "I suppose not. I had never really thought of that. Perhaps this is my very own paradigm shift." Seeing Anna's questioning look, she added, "A fundamental shift or change in the way I look at things."

"I have something for you," Anna said, pulling a

yellowed envelope from her housecoat pocket. "When Zoltan and I took over the inn, we found this, unsealed, unsent, tucked into a Bible in the library. The Mother Superior was working on it at the time she died. I am sharing it with you to perhaps help you believe and understand."

Elizabeth took the outstretched letter. "Thank you. I'll be careful with it."

"Now eat up. A hearty breakfast will ward off you catching the death of a cold from last night!" Anna patted Elizabeth's bed, and then turned to leave the room.

"Anna?"

"Yes?" The old woman faced Elizabeth again.

"What do you know about Josef? I mean, really know about him, who he is, where he's from."

Anna's eyes misted over for a moment. "He will have to tell you."

Elizabeth thought back to his grip on her shoulders, to his eyes, the fierceness in them, and the way he killed the wolf with one upward thrust of his knife. His power was palpable, but so was something else. Mistrust? Pain? "I'll ask him then. And thank you."

"You rest," Anna said softly. "And if you speak to him, know this…I am an old woman, older than you think. I turn seventy-six in April."

Elizabeth's eyes widened. "You look wonderful."

"Hard work and good Slovak food are a good combination. Keeps you young at heart."

Elizabeth smiled. Dumplings were hardly what she'd call heart-healthy.

"In all my years, I have met good men—like Zoltan. And bad men, like the Nazis. I have seen good people in the mountains. And I have seen the handiwork of the devil in the snow. And in all that time, I have never met a man like Josef. He is strong and faithful and honorable. Braver than any soldier."

"That's quite a recommendation."

"Yes. Zoltan and I love him like a son." She nodded, and left the room, shutting the door behind her.

Elizabeth drank from her coffee cup, white porcelain with hawthorn leaves haind-painted around the rim like a wreath. Then she took another bite of kolache—heavenly and sweet. Next she gingerly took the letter from the envelope and unfolded it.

January 17th, 1912
Dear Father Petrochka:
If something should happen to me, I write you, my trusted and faithful friend, to tell you of unspeakable evil. I have lived behind these convent walls for forty years, and the evil has grown, Father. We are here, unable to travel or leave, snowed in, roads blocked by fiends. Daylight—and the Father, Son and Holy Ghost—are our only friends. Hunger is our enemy. And something else, dear Father.

The undead are about us. I fear not so much for my life. I have, after all, lived nearly sixty-seven years. I fear for the sisters here, for their safety if I should be killed.

The undead, I know it sounds strange, but they inhabit the mountains. They encircle the convent at night, making leaving impossible. They have cut off our food supplies. They thirst, Father, for human blood. This can only be the work of Satan himself.

Please, also, one request. If I should become like them, kill me. You will not be

*killing me, your devoted servant in Christ, but
my shell. My soul will be trapped until I am
freed through gruesome death. Tie me to a
strong tree and leave me there for sunrise. I
know, an old woman speaking of such
atrocities, but I assure you, I am very much
aware of Christ and the Cross. Prayers are
always on my lips.*

Oh, and one more thing lest I forget—

Elizabeth shivered. The letter was unfinished.
What could the nuns of the convent have wanted out-
siders to know?

She folded the letter and thought of Josef. Dare
she believe? And if she did, what did that portend for
her brother? Elizabeth's mind drifted to her twin.
She doubted she could ever have the strength to do
as the Mother Superior asked and kill him if...if
what she saw on the mountainside had gotten to him.

Chapter 5

Elizabeth stayed in bed and dozed fitfully until noon. Then she showered, dressed, and found the library, where she pored over books on vampires and one on dhampirs—Anna and Zoltan had quite an unusual book collection. Some of the volumes were dusty and antiquated, Elizabeth presumed from the time the inn was a convent. She suppressed a wry smile imagining what a visiting priest might have thought of the good sisters' reading choices. A good deal were written in Slovak or Czech. Some German.

Some Latin. She searched for ones in languages she could understand. As Elizabeth read, she looked for any credible scholarly support of the existence of vampires and dhampirs, but most of the research was on the fringes or was based on hearsay and superstition and fear.

What she read, however, helped to give her a little education into the lore. From what Elizabeth could tell, vampires weren't just relegated to Dracula and Eastern Europe. In Africa stories of vampires drinking cattle's blood was common—and vampires and undead were an element in many, many cultures. Methods to kill them varied, as did their forms. Wolves were one—but so were bats and black cats and fog and even bears. Dhampirs were, by some accounts, mercenaries. One book said they could not be trusted, and elsewhere in its pages said most were charlatans. Elizabeth shut the volume and fretted. She didn't know what to believe. Her own eyes, or the intellectual knowledge that this was impossible.

Over and over again, Elizabeth thought of what Anna had said about World War II. As a comparative religion professor, Elizabeth was often confronted by students questioning organized religion entirely. They came to her classes searching for answers, and she could offer none. Hers was an academic approach, simply exploring the faiths of the world. She didn't have answers to big questions, the painful ones. Why do bad things happen to good people? Why does God allow children to die? Why did God allow the Holocaust?

That last question was one that tormented her greatly. Like any scholar—particularly one who embraced religious studies and philosophy—the Holocaust stood as the ultimate test of faith. If there indeed was a God, how could he have allowed it? But taking the question a step further, how had human beings, with souls and consciences, have allowed it? Lampshades made from human skin. Mengele's experiments on twins.

As a twin, the infamous experiments disturbed her perhaps that much more. Elizabeth recalled reading a history text as a high school sophmore, tears streaming down her face. Maybe Anna was right. Vampires weren't so difficult to believe in, when compared to the depravity of humanity.

Elizabeth later ate supper with Zoltan and Anna, then went up to bed after promising not to leave the grounds. It was only a half-lie. She didn't promise not to leave the main house—just the grounds. She intended to sneak into Josef's cottage. Just because she saw what seemed to be vampires on the mountainside didn't mean *his* motives could be trusted.

After sunset, around the time he had left his cottage the night before, Elizabeth opened her window just slightly, and peered down at the garden looking for signs that Josef was leaving for the night. She saw him open the door, a sliver of light escaping out into the darkness. Elizabeth watched him part the hawthorn bushes, strangely thrilled by the sight of him. He was the epitome of tall, dark and handsome, she'd give him that. Mysterious, too. But it was again, that indefinable something—a bearing of danger mixed with melancholy, a magnetic energy— that drew her to him.

After she was certain he was gone and off into the mountains, Elizabeth again sneaked downstairs and out through the pantry window. The night air was freezing, and she rubbed her arms as she hurried to the hawthorn bushes. She moved to part them and noticed that many of the branches were cleanly cut. Now she pieced it together. His arrows were hawthorn. He must have made them himself.

Moving aside branches, she stepped through and found herself on the doorstep to his cottage. She tried the worn brass knob on the door and found it turned easily. Holding her breath, she stepped inside.

"Oh my God!" she gasped. A wolf lay across the hearth in front of a dying fire. Elizabeth backed up to the door, prepared to run, but the wolf barely lifted its head in acknowledgment. Standing very still, Elizabeth scrutinized the wolf, and noticed the hair around its eyes and muzzle were almost completely gray. It was old, clearly. Maybe even a half-wolf, for its features seemed less sharp, its muzzle more doglike.

Cautiously, she made her way toward the animal. She held out her hand and it raised its head and licked it. Elizabeth knelt down beside the wolf and whispered, "Okay there, old girl, you won't hurt me. I just want to look around, all right? Then I'll be on my way."

Standing, she surveyed the small room she was in.

In fact, the cottage was a single room, with a sleeping alcove off to the side. The furnishings were simple— a wooden table with four chairs. Elizabeth ran her hand along the table. It was oak and sturdy. It looked hand-hewn. Against one wall stood a Victorian-style sofa with a small table in front of it. Near the fireplace were two rocking chairs. The sleeping alcove contained a double bed, a nightstand and a small wooden altar.

The kitchen was tiny—a refrigerator and a stove and sink. And next to the kitchen, against one wall, was a long wooden table with a shelf above it that clearly functioned as a desk or office. Elizabeth moved over to it and started cautiously moving papers and files slightly, looking for something— anything—that could tell her more about Josef. Something that might lead her to David.

She opened one file folder, and then withdrew her hand in horror. It was full of black and white autopsy photos and crime-scene photos, the pools of blood around victims showing up as midnight ebony syrup. Elizabeth read the labels on the file folders. One after the other were of infamous serial killer cases.

Elizabeth's heart pounded so hard she thought

the wolf would stir from the sound of it. Her ears
rang. Serial killers. He was no dhampir. He was
some sort of blood-lusting killer—or at the very
least some freak fascinated by killers.

Backing away from the table, she decided in an
instant to go to the inn, try to reach her driver, Dima,
and return to Prague. She ran to the door, opened
it…and stood face-to-face with Josef Darecky.

Chapter 6

"Can I help you?" Josef asked, both bemused and angry at the intruder in his cottage.

He saw how flustered—and fearful—she was. "I…I was looking for you."

"Well, here I am." He stepped closer to her, so they nearly touched.

She backed up. "I…was wondering if you were going up into the mountains tonight. But…I'm going to go back to the inn. It's safer there."

"Safer from the vampires…or *me?*" Again he

stepped closer to her, until he could smell the lilies of the valley perfume she wore, and the fear—which he had discovered over the years bore its own scent. It angered him that she would be afraid of him—he saved her life the evening before. The wolf tracking them last night would have definitely slaughtered her—or turned her—had he not been with her. He stared into Elizabeth's eyes. They were so clear, like glacier snow.

"Both," she said. He watched as her eyes darted to his desk.

"In America, isn't what you've done called breaking and entering?"

"No. The door was open. No one answered when I knocked, but the door was unlocked. I…I didn't take anything."

"But you looked through my papers, didn't you? You *spied* on me."

"No!" she snapped, her cheeks turning red and betraying her lie.

"What gives you the right to go through my personal belongings?"

"I'm just desperate to find my brother." He saw her swallow hard with fear.

"You think you have to fear me? Is that it? That I might be like one of them? That I would *ever* be like one of them! Could ever be like them." The idea filled him with revulsion. "Come here." He grabbed her by the arm and pulled her roughly to the desk where he opened a file folder. "Look!" He flung a color crime-scene photo down on the table, the grip on her upper arm still tight. "Anatoy Onopreinko. Ukraine. The police called him The Terminator. Victim after victim. Fifty-two in all."

She winced. *Why did he care so much,* he berated himself. *So what if she was afraid of him, if she thought him a monster.* He knew the truth. But he did care. He wanted those eerie glacier eyes to trust him, not fear him.

Josef let autopsy photos drift down like autumn leaves, covering the table where Elizabeth sank into a chair in horror.

"Andrei Chikatilo. Russia. Fifty-three victims. Liked to *gnaw* on their bodies…. The Colombian child killer. One hundred and forty children. Little girls. Little boys. One hundred and forty. And the world didn't care." He thrust a photo of a child's body up near her face, then let it fall with the rest.

Her eyes were transfixed by the grim photos until it looked like she couldn't bear any more.

"Why are you showing me these?" Her voice was hoarse with emotion. "They're serial killers. Chikatilo…I read about his case in the American press. Serial killers aren't vampires. Why are you so obsessed with them?"

"The police would like you to believe they're serial killers. That they're human. That way you compartmentalize your fear, you tell yourself it's some human anomaly. The work of sociopaths. So you can rest at night. It's the rare work of the insane. The Ted Bundys of the world. You fear them, but at least it's an explanation you can live with. Let me ask you a simple question. Which is harder to believe? A supernatural being who survives by drinking warm blood, that faintly coppery-scented elixir of life…or a living, breathing human who can look upon the pure and innocent faces of a hundred and forty children and murder them? A man who can kill fifty-three women and *feast* on them. Fred West…a serial killer in London, who murdered two of his own daughters as well as numerous prostitutes, hitchhikers and even his ex-wife. Buried them in the concrete for his new patio. The child murders in Belgium. Little girls left in a makeshift dungeon to starve to death. Can you imagine their cries for their mothers…until they stopped crying and came to a dark, dark place where the human heart gives up? Which defies the human mind? An evil that is from a long line of those who went to the dark side, to death and back, in search of immortality, or a human without any semblance of humanity? And if that's the case, is such a person even human anymore? Is there even a soul? These serial killers are vampires who mask their crimes with atrocities to the bodies that disguise their handiwork."

Elizabeth's eyes brimmed with tears. "I don't know what to think," she whispered. "I just know, as a rational human being, that you're asking me to believe in things that make no sense. Like wolves that are vampires."

"Wolves don't stage scenes."

"I beg your pardon?"

He opened another file and tossed several photos at her. "I took these myself."

Elizabeth stared down. Bodies were splayed out on a mountainside, intestines falling into the snow, which was crimson.

"Wolves don't arrange a body facing the moon. Wolves don't paint a circle of blood in the snow. Wolves don't leave marks like this on the neck." He handed her a close-up of one victim. "Even more telling, wolves wouldn't be stopped at holy ground. If I left fresh meat for a hungry wolf, it would come into the convent gardens. My she-wolf isn't afraid of hawthorn. But the wolves in the mountains are. They retreat from it, whimpering."

Elizabeth gazed up at him. She looked as if she might crumble. "What is your story, then, Josef? Who are you? If you want me to believe you are a dhampir, then tell me."

He shut his eyes for a moment and walked over to the hearth where his wolf lay. He bent over and patted her head, scratching behind her ears. He hadn't told his story in so long, and the prospect sent a chill through him.

"She's beautiful," Elizabeth whispered. She stood and approached him.

"She won't hurt you. Her name is Mara." He was grateful for the distraction of his pet, while he tried to decide just what to reveal to the American woman. Zoltan and Anna trusted her. But did he?

"I saw the wolves last night. Are you so sure she's tame?"

"Those from last night are different. Mara is a hybrid. Like me. Half dog, half wolf. I'm half my father, half my mother. Half of the dark, half of the light. She obeys me. She is very loyal. You can pet her."

Elizabeth knelt beside the she-wolf. "We already made friends a little bit. She scared me when I walked in, I thought she was like those other beasts, but I can see she is quite old and gentle."

Elizabeth began gently stroking the wolf's coat. Mara's coat was so thick for winter that Elizabeth's thin, graceful fingers all but disappeared into its fur. Josef found himself longing for Elizabeth to instead touch him. To hold his hand. To not fear him. He spent much of his life as a monster, or at least loathing a part of himself. He wanted her to absolve him of his own genetics.

Glancing over at him, Elizabeth said softly, "I'm sorry I came in here uninvited. It was wrong. I didn't mean to invade your privacy. I just want to find David. That's all. Honestly. I swear it."

He held his hands out to the fire, then took a poker and stoked it, adding a log. Sparks flew up, and he concentrated on the orange tongues of heat. As usual, the cold caused a deep aching in his bones. He sighed and stretched his hands near the flames, flexing and bending his long fingers, trying to keep them from atrophying.

"You can help me, can't you?" the beautiful woman insisted. "Zoltan said you might be able to. If you've seen my brother, you have to help me. Please don't leave him to those monsters on the mountain. I'm begging you."

He wanted to turn her away. To send her back to the main house. He had his own quest, his own reasons for the hunt. But he was equally taken by her beauty and her determination. And maybe what they each wanted wasn't so different from each other.

"If I tell you my story, then you must take a leap of faith. You must not question what I tell you. You're not in the world of academia anymore. You're in *my* world."

At those words, a wolf bayed in the distance.

Elizabeth shuddered and looked at him. "Am I safe here?"

He walked over to his bow and arrow set, and waved at a dagger on the wall. "You are."

"Is my brother all right?"

"I can't be sure."

"Is he with them?" She nodded toward the unopened window in the general direction of the mountain.

"He may be."

"If he is, why was he taken?"

"I'm not sure yet."

"And you really say you are a dhampir?"

"I am."

"Then tell me." She looked him in the eyes. He felt a craving for her. But he pushed that down and moved over to the desk.

"All right. Tonight, your education begins."

Chapter 7

"My mother was killed by vampires." He said it so quietly, Elizabeth had to lean forward to hear him, straining her neck and tilting her head. She sat on the couch and watched him retrieve a file from his desk. She was afraid to breathe, afraid to move, afraid to do anything that might interrupt or scare him off from telling her his story.

"Here…" He handed a manila folder to her, then sat down next to her on the sofa. Being so close to him unnerved her. His eyes were nearly black, and he had a palpable energy about him. Elizabeth sensed that he knew his presence was commanding. He seemed to stand always just a bit too close, as if to gain an advantage by keeping her—his opponent at the moment—unsure of herself.

Elizabeth, hands trembling, took the file and opened it. A police report was on top, which described the murder of a young, single mother, a Czech immigrant living in London with her small son, Josef. She was murdered, the police believed, by drug-crazed junkies. Hacked to death with daggers or ice picks, her blood everywhere—though no murder weapon was ever found.

Elizabeth turned the page and saw crime scene photos that made her feel nauseous. Underneath the last crime-scene photo was a snapshot of a beautiful little boy with black curly hair. He smiled shyly at the camera, but his eyes were blank, sad, surrounded by thick lashes. He clutched a small stuffed animal.

"This is you," she whispered.

Josef nodded, glancing away.

Elizabeth touched his hand. He didn't withdraw it, but she saw him clenching his jaw and saw the muscles in his neck tightening. She felt such an out-pouring of sympathy for him. She and David had lost both their parents, and it colored their lives in a million ways large and small. But murder, slaughter in this way, was unimaginable to her.

Paperclipped next to the photo was another snapshot, this one of an utterly beautiful woman. She was smiling into the camera, a baby in her arms. Her smile was wide, and she had smooth skin and dancing dark eyes.

"Your mother?"

He nodded. "I was there that night." His voice was devoid of emotion, flat, quiet. As if he had practiced repeating these words until he could tell the story without his feelings betraying him.

"My God…" Elizabeth winced slightly. "I can't even begin to imagine."

"My biological father…the undead bastard who raped my mother, of which I am the product, is a vampire. He was the vampire who killed my mother's family, here, in the mountains. She survived, somehow. I never heard the story from her, because I was too young when she died. From what I can piece together from rumors in the nearest village, the vampires attacked her family as they returned home Christmas Eve from visiting relatives in Prague. My mother was brutally raped, but not killed because another car with four soldiers on holiday came upon the scene."

"She lost her entire family?" Elizabeth was always grateful she had David to cling to, which made his disappearance all the more traumatic.

Josef nodded. "She lost her mother, father, sister, brother. It was treated as a serial killer case. She was so traumatized that her claims of the killers drinking her family's blood were ignored. And, like you, she found the truth nearly impossible to believe. She had been raised here. Heard some myths, legends. But she didn't believe. Not really."

"How did she react when she found out she was pregnant?" Elizabeth tried to imagine the young woman, terrified, traumatized, utterly alone, and then the added shock of a pregnancy.

"She fled this country, fled the village where she was looked upon suspiciously as her belly grew a little rounder. She went to England, getting lost among the immigrant population. She got a job keeping house for an older gentleman near Hyde Park. He was very good to her—to both of us. After her death, he established a college fund for me, paid for her funeral. He died maybe fifteen years ago, but I would visit him. He was my surrogate grandfather. He said she adored her pregnancy, patting her belly and smiling every time I kicked. Which was apparently often." He smiled, and Elizabeth suppressed a small smile herself.

"Mr. Hughes was my only source of information about my birth…how she acted during the pregnancy. She didn't ever reveal much about her past, but Mr. Hughes sensed the pregnancy was the first bit of joy she had in a long while. He was struck though, by how alone she was. She had no one. When I was born, he was her only visitor. He spoiled me. He brought teddy bears and blankets and made sure I had a proper crib. He wanted her to come live with him in the Hyde Park house, but she liked her independence. He thought it might also have been whatever it was that made her sad sometimes. He'd hear her, crying, always trying to hide it when he came into the room."

Elizabeth looked down at the picture of the child Josef again. "She must have loved you so very much. Something beautiful to come of so much sadness and grief."

He nodded. "But the vampires found her. She was tied to them via her pregnancy. The more I developed, sharing her blood via the umbilical cord, the stronger the connection. The blood tie is almost like…an insatiable burning, like a heroin addict going through withdrawls. It's a craving, an evil calling, a homing device. She could feel them, had visions, hallucinations, of their slaughters."

Elizabeth blanched. "Hallucinations?"

"Yes."

Elizabeth thought of the marks she had seen on her neck in Prague. They had looked so real. Then she noticed her hand was still covering his. She wondered what it meant to be half-vampire, and yet even as she wondered, she questioned her own sanity. How could she take this all at face value?

"Do you remember the night…that she was killed?"

"I wish I didn't, but I do. I heard it all, smelled the scent of blood. Her blood. She hid me in a trunk, and so my other senses—not sight—are what recall the murder. I'm like a shark. A drop of blood, and I smell it, recall that night. It brings me back to the one night I wish I could forget."

"Did your mother know you were a dhampir? Did she know what that meant?"

"She was from a rural area out here. She knew. She knew this inn. I am sure she dismissed some of the stories about what happened to the nuns as myth, as superstition. Legend. But when it came true. When she saw them feast on her family, then yes, she knew."

Elizabeth watched his lips as he spoke. They were full. He had high slashes of cheekbones, and he had a small cleft in his chin. He was unshaven, which only added to his mystique, his aura of world-weariness.

"Anna says you suffer. What does she mean? That night? The memory of that night?"

"That. But physically. Dhampirs usually are born with bone problems. The bones fuse incorrectly *in utero*. Usually, their bodies are twisted, misshapen—if they survive the painful journey out through the birth canal—and most don't. I was born by caesarean section, and in my case, my bones were fine. It's my joints, my spine. My affliction is as if I have severe rheumatoid arthritis—without the swelling so much, but with all the pain and stiffness magnified a hundredfold."

"Can you be treated?" She tried to avoid staring. Part of her was looking, she guessed, for signs he was half beast, like some fairy-tale monster.

"No. I've tried. My adoptive parents tried every avenue to help me. My surrogate grandfather in Hyde Park spared no expense. Took me to the major children's hospital on Ormond Street. But it wasn't as if at that time anyone knew what I had. And even if Mr. Hughes had known, how could he have told a doctor? No, I suffer. Not only did I have the trauma of what I lived through, the loss of my mother, the pain of dhampirism, but also, as part of my father, I received the so-called gift of extraordinary senses. I can see vampires where others don't. I can hear them, smell them. Noises imperceptible to you became like bombs going off to me. It was impossible for me to attend normal school until I learned to deal with it."

"Did your adoptive parents…what did they know about your parentage? I mean…who were they?"

"The police detective who plucked me from the trunk where I was hiding was a deeply honorable man. Very smart. Well-read. Loved his wife, Beatrice, so incredibly. And they couldn't have children though they wanted them desperately. He said he loved me from the moment I wrapped my arms around his neck. They adopted me. But like all good police detectives, he operated on what he saw, on the facts—as well as instinct. And something told him all was not quite right with that police report you're holding. There had to be more to the story. And the more he looked into my mother's past, as well as witnessed my pain— my physical pain and my unusual sensory percep- tions—the more he was certain something unnatural was at work. He didn't come to that conclusion easily. As a police detective, he believed in this world—the visible one we all take for granted. But he was able to see to the evil around him. A detective finding clues."

"So was he able to figure out who your father was?"

"He and I, as I got older, were able to piece by piece put it all together. My mother—my adoptive mother— passed away when I was in high school. I will always, of course, mourn my biological mother, but I was blessed with a loving adoptive mother who was utterly and completely kind. She died of cancer, and we—my adoptive father and I—were at her bedside when she took her last breath. Eventually, my father and I made plans to come to the Czech Republic to see if we could destroy my biological father, destroy vampires. By this time, we had amassed a huge number of files and cases of serial killers we were convinced were actually undead. It was our theory. Our life's work."

"So you came to the inn?"

"Not right away. He and I perfected our killing strategies. We were like everyone who has ever read vampire lore or seen a vampire movie. We tried to find them in their coffins during daylight. But though freshly turned vampires are weak and still adjusting to their undead status, those who have years—or centuries—of killing beneath their belts are devilishly clever."

"You couldn't find them?"

"Sometimes we did, but we even encountered one who had hired mercenaries to guard his sleeping spot by day. He paid them in prostitutes, drugs and money to keep them loyal."

"So when did you turn to the hawthorn?"

"Early on. We hoped that the hawthorn arrows would allow us to kill them at night, from a distance. We used hawthorn arrows, as well as hawthorn stakes, but at first, we were unschooled, unpracticed. Our human instincts weren't vicious. We weren't killers. Not by training, not by nature. Eventually, though, we were able to kill several vampires. But then my adoptive father was captured."

He looked away, withdrew his hand from hers, and stood and walked over to the fire. He started speaking with his back to her. "I presume they have killed him. I was careless during a hunt. We both were. We still didn't quite know what we were up against. I came to the inn to nurse my wounds and ended up staying. I became as good an archer as an Olympian. I trained until I couldn't be beaten. And Zoltan and Anna needed me, and they, in turn, gave me the cottage. All of which brings me to you, tonight."

He turned around and approached the couch again. Elizabeth was very aware of how close he was, how tall. Again, she wondered, was part of him beast-like? She had seen his fury on the mountainside, seen him draw a dagger. She was scared of him, and yet her heart broke for a man, a boy, who had experienced so much loss and pain in his life.

"Can I ask you something?" Josef said.

She looked up and nodded.

"Do you think I'm a freak?"

Elizabeth searched for the right words. "I'm scared. I'm scared to be here…an ocean away from my life, searching for my brother, in a place where wolves stage bodies in the moonlight, with a man who tells me he is half-vampire. But I—" She stared straight into his eyes.

"What?"

"I believe you."

"Well, that's a start now, isn't it?"

"Will you help me find David? Will you?"

"If you promise to obey me. I can't have you in danger. I lost my adoptive father. I don't want to lose anyone else. It's why I live and work alone."

"*Obey* you?" She bristled at the suggestion.

His pupils contracted then widened. "You have no choice. I'm the one who knows about the vampires."

Elizabeth clenched her jaw. "Fine."

"Good. Now tell me more about your brother."

Reluctantly, irritated by his smugness, astounded at how he infuriated her, Elizabeth began to talk.

Chapter 8

Josef sat down on the couch, close to her. He wasn't sure why he liked making her uncomfortable, but he did. A part of him hated her because she was so beautiful and she would never be his. Not fully. She was wholly human, and he had the mark of the beast. The part of him he loathed and despised would always make a woman like Elizabeth fear him.

However, as he looked at her, saw how she regarded him with compassion more than terror, he was relieved. He had told the worst of his story, and she hadn't run from him. Not yet, at least. So maybe that was why, he mused, he tried to unnerve her. To push her away before her fears made her run away.

"My brother David is a writer, an artist, the most creative person I know. He can tell a joke, whip up a gourmet meal, he's well-read, a philosopher…women love him, and men want to be his friend. He's got a dark side. We all do, I suppose. He's been in rehab, dabbled in drugs. But he was past that period in his life. He had moved on. He's my best friend and sounding board, and he went missing in Prague."

"Parents?" Josef settled back against the couch, letting his arm drape near the nape of her neck. He took his index finger and touched her throat ever so slightly, then stopped, watching her flush.

"Um…parents." She exhaled. "Well, our mother died when we were small."

"Do you remeber her?" Josef had so few memories of his mother, they were like fragments of glass, splintered and fragile, yet piercing.

"Not very well. She was lovely. Beautiful. She adored us, but she was in a head-on accident. My father was teaching a semester at Yale. A drunk driver hit her. She died immediately. But to us children, she disappeared. One day, David and I were like everyone else. We had a mother and a father and sat down to eat together. And the next she was gone, and after a while, we could remember so little of her, I almost used to feel as if I had perhaps made her up, like a fairy tale. After she died, our father was mad."

"Angry?"

"No, mad. Insane. Crazy. However you want to term it." She waved her hand in the air. "He was a brilliant man. IQ off the charts. Same as David."

"And you." He said it as fact. He could tell she was brilliant, quick-minded.

She blushed bright red. "Yes. Same as me. But my father was always in his head, in his math proofs. We were gypsies—moving from university to university. He never got tenure. They used him to add some bit of glamour to their math departments—he was a legend in the field—but everyone knew he was too unstable to teach regularly. When he would lose it, we were off to the next university. Until he finally killed himself. I found his body."

Josef was silent. His pain was always so present. There was no escaping the physical agony, the spiritual emptiness, the mourning. But certainly she knew pain as well.

"I'm sorry." He withdrew his arm from the back of the couch. He didn't want to scare her anymore. Now he wanted to comfort her.

"What I don't understand is how my brother, a world traveler, intelligent, sensible, street smart, could have fallen prey to them."

"I am less concerned with how—they are quite cunning—and more concerned with why. They clearly chose him."

"*Chose* him?"

Josef nodded. "You saw the village woman. They could have turned her or simply fed on her. They fed on her and discarded her carcass. They wouldn't have given it a thought. Turning is more of a…blood tie, if you will. Your brother, when he passed through, was ill. Sickness, weakness…they had partially turned him, I think. I didn't speak with him. Zoltan and Anna did and reported to me, but by the time I went to the main house to investigate, he had left—I think the hawthorn was already becoming too much for him. Even in winter when it's dormant, the sight of it is terrifying to the turned."

"I can't imagine why they would choose him. I know him better than anyone. Twins are like that. I innately know what he thinks before he thinks it."

Twins. She had referred to him all this time as her brother, not her twin. How had he missed it? Josef stood up excitedly and crossed the room to the bookshelf, pulling down what looked like an ancient diary.

"Here." He thrust it at her.

"What am I looking at? I can't read this."

He laughed. "I forgot you might not read Slovak."

"I don't speak Czech either. I'm lucky to get by with English, French, Latin—oh, so useful in conversation—a smattering of ancient Greek, and enough Spanish to get by when I travel."

"Well, what you're looking at is a diary explaining vampire lore and written by a vampire hunter in the early eighteenth century. According to old legends in what's now the Czech Republic, twins have a special ability, sometimes, to be able to see and sense vampires."

"Twins?"

"I regarded it, frankly, as more superstition than truth. Women pregnant with twins would have been far more likely to die during childbirth before modern medicine. Even today it's considered a high-risk pregnancy. So perhaps twins were regarded as bad luck. Touched by the dark side. Conceived through evil."

"But I've never been able to detect vampires. I don't have some special ability to see them."

"Have you ever looked for them? Ever even tried?"

"Of course not!" Her eyes radiated anger.

"I told you, if you want to enter my world, leave your preconceived notions behind."

He sat down next to her again. "My biological father, the leader of this vampire clan, lives even deeper in the mountains near some ruins of an ancient castle—I think. I've always lost the trail deep in the forest. But what I do know of him is this. He longs to be the most powerful vampire ever. It's not enough for him to be immortal, to live forever. He wants to be immortal in legend. For his name to be associated with terror. As such, he'll kill or destroy anyone who stands in his way, with dhampirs and seers—twins who can detect vampires—high on his list. Perhaps he somehow discerned your brother was a twin. Or maybe he saw your picture in your brother's wallet. Maybe he wants to mate with you. He has carnal desires even if he's undead. I think he craves sex to feel powerful. It's certainly not love or even lust."

"Rape never is."

"We cannot guess, but mark my words, he has some use for you—or he wants to destroy you. And that is what is keeping your brother alive or in some suspended state, however tenuously, not quite turned, for now. The vampire is luring you to your brother."

She clutched her stomach. "This is all really overwhelming, Josef."

"Let me ask you, have you and your brother ever been able to communicate with one another without speaking?"

She looked away. "Yes."

"Why aren't you looking at me? What aren't you telling me?"

She bowed her head. "When we were little, we had a secret language. But often we didn't even need that. Any time something horrible happened, like the night my father killed himself, we've had those strange coincidences people sometimes talk about. The night my father sat in his car, locked, in the garage, engine running, I was in the library. David— being David—was in a pub. At pretty much the precise moment we were told our father would have entered the car, I suddenly packed up my books, David put down his beer, and we went searching for each other. He found me in my dorm as I was getting ready to go to *his* dorm. Once we were certain each other was all right, we just knew. David went to my father's office. I raced home and found my dad…his body. By the time David got there, I didn't even need to speak."

"Maybe it was not such a coincidence as you think."

"It's happened so many times in our lives, that we take it for granted." She paused. "When I arrived in Prague, I had a nightmare, a bad dream, of two marks here." She touched her neck.

He moved closer to her, his breath near her throat. She flinched.

"Are you afraid of me?"

"No," she said stiffly.

"Look at me," he commanded.

Slowly, she turned to him.

"When you look in my eyes, do you see something inhuman? Something undead? You said you never saw vampires before, but you weren't looking. Now, I want you to see me as I am. Half of me. My dark side. Look in my eyes and what do you see?"

She stared deeply into his eyes. They sat there, inches from each other's faces, for what seemed to Josef like minutes. He ached for her, and that totally puzzled him. He had never longed for a woman before, mostly because he so hated his dark half that it drove him further and further from human contact.

"The only thing I see," she said quietly, "is a good soul who has suffered. I don't see a part-vampire. I see *you*, Josef."

He leaned in to taste her, to kiss her, but thought better of it. If they hunted together, being involved with her would only make him lose his edge. If he came across her brother, and David was fully turned,

Josef had to slaughter him, no matter if she was beside him or not.

It was his destiny to be alone forever.

Chapter 9

Elizabeth was confused. "What's the matter?"

"Nothing."

"Was that the wrong answer? Did you *want* me to see something dark and demon-like in you?"

"No." He refused to look at her.

"I think you *want* to hate that side of yourself. I think you're like anyone else refusing to make peace with their dark side."

"My dark side is a little more complex than that. My dark side is inhuman. It's undead."

She placed a hand on his chest. "You're not undead. Your heart beats humanly. You feel for people, for your mother and your adoptive father. For Zoltan and Anna. You hunt not to thrill seek, not because you're a sociopath or cruel, but to do the right thing. To rid the world of this scourge that took your mother."

"I'm evil."

"You're not. You're like anyone else whose father is a murderer or rapist or abuser. You may have his blood, his DNA, but that doesn't make you the man you are, Josef. Your adoptive parents saw to that. Those years with your mother, those years of her nursing you and cradling you, those years can't be erased by DNA. By your biology. It's nature *and* nurture. You have *her* genes in you, too."

"But his genes are what sicken me."

"Our father—David's and mine—was insane. All our lives we've feared it. Feared that our IQs doomed us to repeat his history. Children of the mentally ill feel a sense of shame. I felt it. embarrassed when my father sank into a depression and we couldn't have our friends over. But I am my own person. I refuse to go down that path."

Without warning, he pulled her to him. His chest was against her breasts, smashing them roughly.

Their lips were so close if she moved an inch forward, they would touch.

"If I kissed you right now, your first thought would be that you were kissing a dhampir. If my lips were cold, you would wonder if that was the undead part of me."

"If you kissed me right now," she said evenly, "I would think you a man."

"You would always think of my biology. You would always wonder."

She shook her head. And to prove it, she leaned in and kissed him.

His return kiss stunned her to her core. She had never in her entire life been kissed with such fury. He was hungry for her; she felt that. He kissed her mouth roughly, but then pulled back and sensuously licked her lips, then bit them gently, then kissed her with that indescribable longing again.

She lost her breath. In the pit of her stomach, in the place that had so rarely been awakened fully before, she felt her own furious hunger for him. After a lifetime of unfulfilling relationships, men who were kind and good and decent and handsome, but not, somehow, the *one,* she had traveled across the globe to find him. She was sure of it. Him. Josef. A man not quite a man and not a beast. A hunter. Otherwise, how to explain the connection?

He moved his lips to her neck. Slowly, he inched his way to her nape, and then moved her sweater slightly to nibble along her collarbone.

Elizabeth exhaled, feeling as if she had never totally surrendered to a lover until this moment.

He turned his attention to her ear, whispering, "I want you."

"Josef, I want you, too."

She took his face in her hands, her fingertips on his cheekbones. She kissed one eyelid, then the other, then his lips. She held his face firmly, forcing him to look at her intently.

"I see a man I want when I look deeply into your eyes. That's what I see. A man."

He stood in one swift movement and pulled her into his arms, carrying her to the sleeping alcove. Elizabeth smiled slightly as they passed the she-wolf on the hearth, who lifted her head in curiosity, then resumed sleeping.

Josef laid Elizabeth down on his bed. Outside, she could hear the wind—the night was cold. But the bed had a goosedown cover and flannel sheets, and a small wood-burning, cast-iron stove glowed slightly in the corner.

Josef lifted her sweater, licking her stomach. She pulled off the sweater entirely, her nipples hard from the cold and his touch.

"Let's get under the covers," he said, stripping out of his black sweater and pants, as she unbuttoned her own jeans and slid out of them. When he was standing in his boxers, Elizabeth was awed by his physique, toned and muscular, a dark line of hair sexily creating a path from his stomach down into his boxers.

He looked down at her, braless, in just panties, lying on the goosedown comforter, which billowed up on either side of her.

"I have never seen anyone more beautiful in my life," he said huskily.

"I want you inside me."

"Let me lick you first. Let me taste you."

He knelt down and slowly removed her panties,

then kissed his way up her thighs. He lifted one leg and kissed behind her knee, an erogenous zone she didn't even know she had. She shuddered as his lips moved up higher, finally tasting her, first in small nibbles, then in fervent teasing flicks of his tongue that literally sent her reeling and sliding back away from him.

Josef moved aside the covers, and took off his boxers. He was already erect, and Elizabeth leaned up on one elbow and playfully licked his cock.

When he slid under the covers next to her, she thought just feeling his stomach against her belly, feeling him full against her would send her over the edge. His touch made her that crazy with desire.

The next moments were a frenzy. She wanted to slow down, wanted to remember each moment with him, this perfect lover, but it became a forceful tangle, him pulling on her hair, she biting against his chest.

"I want you," she said, feeling as if he did not enter her *that* moment that she would die of some unfulfilled lust.

He looked down at her. His eyes were black in the darkness, and he was breathless. "I've never felt anything like this before. I swear..." He nuzzled her neck.

He slid into her and both of them moaned at once. He slid out. "Elizabeth...I really care for you. I feel something between us."

"I do, too." There it was again, no empty encounter, but some connection.

He slid inside her again, and their bodies fit together perfectly. He filled her—body and heart. He moved faster and faster, and she felt herself rising to a crescendo.

"Oh, my God." She bit his shoulder. "I want to come together."

"Don't wait for me."

"No." She bit him again. She was close to tears from the near-release of this passion she felt for him.

He moved in and out, and she gave him cues with her moaning. Finally, they were there on the threshold together. She gave a small scream, and then he moaned and collapsed against her, breathing heavily.

For the first time in her life, Elizabeth saw stars. Real stars in front of her eyes in a sparkling array.

She was dizzy, and if she had been asked to stand at that moment, she wouldn't have been able to, she was certain.

He kissed her long and hard, then softer. "I'm not done with you, angel."

She was shocked to find she wasn't done with him either. The second time, he moved slower, teasing her more, kissing her to orgasm.

"Let me make you feel good, Josef," she said, climbing on top of him, then nibbling her way down his stomach. She playfully stuck her tongue in his belly button, then kissed further down. He was hard already.

"That is just from hearing you come," he whispered. Then he exhaled loudly. "God, Elizabeth, you do things to me."

She continued her mission to make him beg for her. She had never delighted so much in giving a man pleasure.

"Please, darling," he said. "Let me go inside you."

She straddled him, and slid his hardness between her legs. Again, the instant he was inside of her, she felt a furious passion. The two of them rocked up and down, in and out, enjoying prolonging the pleasure until they again felt in synch.

"Go ahead," he said. "Oh, God…"

Again, they reached their orgasms simultaneously, as if they had been lovers for years, knowing each other's secrets, Elizabeth mused. Maybe what he said about twins being seers was true, but more than that perhaps somehow seers and dhampirs were destined for each other.

She collapsed onto his chest, letting her hair tease his face. He brushed it aside. "If I never left these four walls again, and only made love to you, ate and slept, forever, I don't think I would ever grow tired of you. I'd never want to leave."

"Me either." Unexpectedly, she felt the tears she held back welling in her eyes.

"What's wrong? Elizabeth, what's wrong?"

"Nothing. It's just with you, this between us, it's perfect. I never had this before, love."

"What did you say?" He brushed a stray tear from her cheek.

"Hmm?" she murmured.

"What did you call me?"

She hesitated, shrugging, feeling foolish for using the word as a term of affection, even if she inexplicably felt it.

"Whatever this is makes no sense. None at all. But this is something only the fates could have dreamed up."

She looked down at him, picturing for a brief moment, the little boy in the photo. Maybe they had both been broken-hearted their whole lives, grieving and waiting for the other to make them whole.

"I feel the same."

She slid down next to him and nestled against his arm. She didn't want to fall asleep. She wanted to stay awake all night making love. He stroked her arms, and she ran her fingers in feathery brushes across his belly. And eventually, sometime in the darkness, as the fire in the fireplace burned lower and extinguished, and the wood-burning stove lost its red and orange embers, she fell asleep.

Chapter 10

He heard her scream.

She was sitting upright in bed, covers clutched to her breasts, shrieking.

"My God, Elizabeth!" He struggled to alertness, mildly shocked to find a beautiful woman in his bed, remembered the night of total sexual energy, and wrapped his arms around her. When she still screamed, he shook her slightly. "It's me. Josef."

She sobbed, unable to talk. Her mouth opened but

a wracking cry escaped her lips, and her forehead was hot, feverish.

"What, baby, what?" He held her to him, tighter. He loved the feel of her in his arms, as if she was sculpted or created for just that spot.

"Listen…" she finally managed to say.

He could hear the wolves. They were howling with an intensity he had never witnessed in his two years at the inn. He kissed the top of her head, then grabbed her face in his hands and kissed away the tears.

"The wolves? Is that what scared you? They won't come on sacred ground. We're always safe here."

She shook her head. "It's not just that. I had a dream. About David." She was now breathing in and out heavily, the way a little girl might after a bad dream.

"What happened in it? Try to remember everything."

She squinted her eyes shut. "He was in a dungeon. A cave or a dungeon. It was dark and very cold. I couldn't see him, but I could hear him breathing heavily. He was terrified. He could hear them feeding above him, or maybe in the next room. It sounded like a frenzy. And they kept telling him he would be next.... And then they came in, and he thought it was his death. But instead, they brought him down a long corridor to a woman. She was..." Elizabeth shook her head furiously, her black hair wild and carefree from their night of lovemaking. "I can't say it."

"You have to. Tell me," he insisted. He was convinced, in that moment, that she was envisioning things *exactly* as they occurred. She was a seer, through her brother's eyes. That was why she could see the walls, sense his terror—but not see her twin's face.

"They..." She clutched her sides. "They took him to a woman who was naked and chained to a wall. Someone held up a lantern. Water dripped around the prisoner. She was shivering. Her neck was already bleeding, and they led him to her. They told him to drink or die. Right there. Right then. He refused." She looked at Josef, her voice insistent. "You must know he refused. He was kicking and screaming himself. So they shoved his face up to her neck and forced the blood down his throat. I could taste it. I could feel David retching. And then..." She exhaled. "Then the leader, he grabbed David's face and looked at him, but he was looking through David and into *me*. And he said he was going to find us."

"Us?"

"He said, 'I'll find you.' He said 'you,' but don't ask me how, I knew he meant *us*. You and me."

Josef watched as she wiped her face with her fists.

"I'll get him before that ever happens."

She sniffled. "You don't understand. I came here to find David, not to find love. I'm torn between finding them and wanting to hide from them. I want us both to leave and go to Virginia, and nestle in my own bed at the foot of the Blue Ridge, and just forget this whole insane world I've stumbled into. None of this can really be happening. But it is. And much as I want to run away, I can't leave him here to become one of them. I can't."

"We won't. I'll find your brother." Even as he said it, he realized he had seriously gotten himself in deep. Hours ago, he had told himself that he couldn't fall for her because if he had a choice to make, he would destroy her brother. Now he was promising a rescue mission.

"Make love to me. Make it go away just until

morning," she begged. "Make the dream go away." Her voice was so desperate, begging, anguished. It sent a pang through him.

He didn't want to tell her that her bad dream was probably David's reality. Tenderly, he took his hands and pushed her gently down on the bed. He decided to kiss every inch of her. "Roll over," he whispered.

She rolled onto her belly, and he started with the nape of her neck and worked his way down to the cleft of her ass. He kissed her and nibbled, whispering, "I'm here, it's going to be okay." He spoke soothingly, trying to calm her. When he felt her body relax, he rolled her over, bringing her to orgasm again. Every time he heard her slightly high-pitched "Oh, my God," he felt as if he would come himself.

He slid into her and made love to her slowly, bringing her to orgasm again. This time, when he came, it was he who collapsed on her. Then he dug his elbows into the mattress to support himself, and brought his face to hers, so close, his lips just about touched hers.

"Do you believe in soul mates?" he asked.

"I didn't," she whispered. "Not before. But I do now."

"Do you trust me?"

"Yes."

He wanted more than ever to not face morning. In his entire life, he had experienced few lovers. His affairs were very rare and short-lived, and never intense. He held his heart back, refusing to surrender it. After a time, he assumed his dhampirism doomed him not only to a life of pain but a life of loneliness. The thought made him bitter, but then after bitterness came resignation and after that, a sort of existential angst magnified by the incessant hunt for vampires and dealing with death all the time. He imagined he wasn't much different from long-time cops or morgue workers, combating death with a dark humor and an edge, with a cold, flat response to what he usually saw.

"I'll bring David back to you."

"But what if he's become one of them?"

Josef was silent.

She wriggled slightly, pushing him up a little bit. "Tell me. Tell me what it is you don't want to say."

"If he's turned, then the only way to free him is to kill him. Then his soul, if you believe in a soul, will move on from his body and its undead existence. If he's only half-turned, I can free him by killing his sire. And his sire is very powerful. Killing him will not be easy."

She bit her lip, but he saw in her eyes resoluteness, clearly the eyes of a daughter who had lost both her parents, who wandered from university to university with a mentally unstable father, coming through it with her intelligence and inner strength. "I'm coming with you."

"No, you're not."

"Yes, I am."

He took her wrists and pinned her arms down, then lowered himself to her lips. "No."

She fought against him. "Please, Josef. He's my brother. My twin. That's why I even had this vision. What you said is true. I must be a seer. I can help you."

"But I won't let you."

"Why?"

"Isn't it obvious? I've lost all the people in the world I've loved. If I lost you, then I couldn't face living. I couldn't."

He released her arms and put his face down on her shoulder, kissing her. He felt unwanted and very unfamiliar tears sting his eyes, and he most definitely didn't want her seeing that. He forced the pain in his chest further down. How could he possibly describe to her what it felt like to make love to her?

"Josef, usually when two people meet, they keep their vulnerabilities hidden." She rolled onto her side facing him. They were now face-to-face, and she stroked his cheekbone. "We haven't done that. I'm here, desperate to find my brother. You're here, desperate to exterminate evil. We're two people on the edge of something dark and dangerous. And we're two people who accidentally have found ourselves on the edge of something utterly unexpected and perfect."

He watched her speak. Her lips formed a perfect cupid's bow, and in the dark, he could make out her pale eyes and porcelain skin.

"Unexpected is right," he whispered. He ached for her already. "I'm laying all my cards on the table, Elizabeth. I don't have time for bullshit. Not now. Not with wolves baying in the distance."

He leaned in and kissed her.

She kissed him back. "I never felt this way. I've never made love this way. I've never physically felt a *pain,* an acute and awful *pain,* at the thought of leaving someone's bed. I've never had someone enter me and feel my soul leave me. None of this. And I can't send you alone to face this. I can't and I won't. We won't ever move on and be together and perfect like this moment unless we kill the beast who raped your mother and stole away my brother. And we either do it together or I leave and go into the forest alone."

"That's crazy talk, Elizabeth. Sheer insanity. They'd feed on you the first night." He could think of a hundred reasons why he could never allow it. More than a hundred. He thought of all his and his father's files—his adoptive father who would always be his *real* father. If there were four hundred murders, five hundred, attributable to the beasts in Europe, more…a thousand, then he could add that as a thousand more reasons on top of the personal ones— that he simply loved her and couldn't let her fight the vampires with him. But the thought of her making good on her threat, that terrified him most of all.

"I will live with you forever or die with you in the mountains. But I won't watch you leave for a hunt without me. I won't be a…widow…to these creatures."

"Do you realize how foolish this is, Elizabeth? How dangerous?"

"When you're inside me, Josef, it's all I can do to keep from crawling inside of you, from devouring you. From meshing you into my body and making us one person."

And there he was, hard again. "All right" he heard himself agreeing. "Tomorrow I start training you. And you must learn everything as I did. Fast. You must do whatever I say."

"You must do whatever I say." Her voice was playful yet husky.

"All right," he teased. "What is your command, mistress?"

"I'll whisper it in your ear, once you're inside me."

He slid inside of her. Then she leaned close to his ear. "I want to hear you beg to come."

"Beg?" he asked, desire in his voice.

"Mmm-hmm." She rose up to meet him and then slid him all the way out. Up again, knocking the breath out of him.

"Please," he whispered. "Don't make me come yet." Begging felt too vulnerable.

"No. Beg me to *let* you come."

She rose up to meet him again, then pulled him out.

He wanted to refuse, but then he felt her lips on his neck. Cold from the room made him shiver, and then her kisses drove him mad.

"Please, Mistress Elizabeth, let me."

"That's a good boy," she teased. "But you're really the one in control…I'm yours."

"Then we're both slaves to love," he said, as he sank into her and into ecstasy.

Chapter 11

Morning came too early, Elizabeth mused. She lay there, facing the wood-burning stove, replaying the night's lovemaking in her mind. She smiled to herself. All her life, she had been jealous of that strange bubble those truly in love inhabit. She was annoyed by the almost haughty sense lovers had that their passion was unique. And yet here she was, in Josef's bed, thinking that no one, ever in history, had so sexually and spiritually felt this way. No one had ever had an orgasm so fierce; no one had ever wanted to die rather than be apart from their lover the way she felt. She knew how naive and foolish and insanely in lust that sounded, and yet she meant it and felt it.

She rolled over to kiss him, imagining morning lovemaking followed by breakfast, and discovered an empty bed.

"Josef?" She sat up alarmed. What if he had gone into the mountains alone? She would be furious—and she would follow him. How dare he!

"Josef!" she called out more sharply. She got no response and felt a fury like a hot stone in her gut. Then she saw the bathroom door was half open. She climbed from bed, pulled on his sweater from the night before. It fell below her ass, and provided some warmth. Even better, as she lifted a sleeve to her face, it smelled of him.

"Josef?" She walked to the bathroom, and heard something…a moan. She pushed the door open and saw him lying on his side, knees drawn up, on the floor. "Oh, my God, darling, what is it? What is it?" Panic spread through her, and her hands instantly began shaking. Her teeth chattered. "You're scaring me. What's wrong?"

Pain had caused him to turn a ghostly pale. He was sweating, and she could tell he was breathing shallowly. "I don't want you to see me like this," he whispered. "Please…I don't want you to see me. Go back to the inn."

"No!" She turned and ran to the bed and pulled the comforter from it, dragging it across the floor to his side. She covered his body, naked except for boxers, then cradled his head in her lap, wrapping his curls around her fingers, and stroking his cheek. "Is this what it's like? Every day?"

"Sometimes." He grimaced. "Sometimes the mornings are so bad, I pass out from the pain. I didn't expect last night to happen. I never wanted anyone to see me this way. I don't want you to." His voice grew sharp.

"What can I do to help you?"

"Nothing!"

"I can touch you. I can be here for you."

He shut his eyes. "I hate my dhampirism. I hate what I am."

Elizabeth touched his lips with her finger. "Rest." She pulled off the sweater, and lay down next to him, spooning him. She pressed her breasts against his back, which was hot to the touch, and pulled the covers up over the two of them. Then she simply put her cheek against his neck and periodically kissed him, waiting for him to gather the strength to get up off the floor.

She wasn't sure how long they lay there together, but after some time, he managed to raise himself up on one elbow. "I can make it to bed now," he said, his voice gravelly and drained.

She helped pull him up to standing, and together they inched their way to the bed. He sat down, and she tucked him in. "I'll go up to the main house and get us some breakfast. I'll ask Anna for some of her poultices or herbal remedies, okay?"

He nodded weakly. His eyes were sunken, with dark circles beneath them, his lips parched and cracked.

Elizabeth pulled on her jeans from the night before, her socks, and her boots. She'd get a change of clothes at the inn. Better yet, she'd gather her things and come stay at the cottage. Bending down to kiss him, she left, passing Mara on the hearth. "Watch over him, girl, okay?"

Stepping out into the frigid morning air, Elizabeth's breath instantly formed a cloud of vapor in front of her. Fresh snow crunched under her boots, and she folded her arms across her chest, and tromped across the grounds to the main house, which was shrouded in fog. She entered through the front door where she was greeted by a bemused Anna.

"Up awfully early today," Anna said, giving Elizabeth a mock-stern look.

"Yes, Anna." Elizabeth smiled despite herself. "It's true, I spent the night at Josef's cottage."

"That's good!" Anna replied firmly, nodding her head. "He has been so lonely."

Elizabeth nodded. "But now I need your help. He's sick, Anna. Very weak. In a lot of pain."

The old woman clucked. "I'll get a tray together and come right down to the cottage. We'll get him feeling better. You go on up and freshen up, shower. I'll make a wonderful breakfast and bring it to the two of you in the cottage along with my remedies."

"Thank you," Elizabeth said gratefully. She ran up the main staircase toward her room, pausing at the hawthorn stained glass window. "Please help him," she entreated, thinking of the sisters and offering up a silent prayer.

Once in her room, she opened the dresser drawers and threw her clothes on the bed. Then she grabbed her thick winter Turkish terrycloth robe and crossed the hallway to the bathroom, took a fast shower, towel-dried her hair, and pulled it into a ponytail. She looked at herself closely in the mirror. Did she look different, she wondered. Between the vampires on the mountaintop and the incredible night with Josef, she felt she would never be the same.

Back in her room, she changed into fresh jeans and heavy wool socks, boots, and a black turtleneck and thick wool fisherman's sweater over that. She looked at Josef's black sweater lying on the bed and lifted it up and rubbed her cheek against it. Why did he have to suffer so much?

She grabbed the dress hanging in the closet, tossed her belongings into her suitcase, zipped the suitcase shut, and headed downstairs. Zoltan was in the cavernous foyer.

"Leaving us, I see?"

"I'm going to stay at the cottage with Josef," she replied, blushing slightly. After all, things had moved ridiculously quickly. But he *needed* her.

"Do you want some help carrying that over? I can bring it later and leave it on his doorstep."

"No, that's all right. It's not too terribly heavy." Elizabeth hefted the bag and stepped back outside into the cold. As she stood there looking up at the gray sky, she had a moment of deep doubt. He hadn't invited her to stay, and here she was showing up, baggage and all. Well, he would just *have* to let her stay. She was going to find her brother with him, and they were going to have to work together anyway.

Trudging through the snow, she looked up at the sky. The mountains rivaled the Alps for beauty, though today their peaks were hidden, ominous. How could a place of such majesty contain such dark secrets? She walked on and reached the cottage. She opened the door and saw him in the sleeping alcove, dressed in plaid flannel paĵama bottoms and a T-shirt, resting up against a couple of pillows. He was still dreadfully pale.

She set her suitcase down and shut the door, then walked to the alcove, took off her boots, and slid onto the bed next to him.

"I see you brought your suitcase," he said, smiling wryly.

"Well, I thought you might not mind the company." She kissed his cheek, which was rough with dark stubble, giving him the appearance of a macho action hero, she mused.

"This morning didn't scare you off?"

"No." She slipped her hand under the covers and found he was hard. "I see your weakness hasn't affected everything," she teased.

"No," he growled. "Not everything." He moaned slightly as he adjusted himself in bed so he could wrap an arm around her as she stroked him.

"We must behave," she said. "Anna is coming with breakfast and her remedies."

"Good. She's a saint. I'll be feeling stronger in no time."

"Then tomorrow we can train?"

He sighed. "I had hoped with the light of day, you'd think better of your plan."

"No. I'm only more determined."

"I was afraid of that. And yet I'm equally certain I won't be able to change your mind."

A knock on the door interrupted their discussion. "Come in," Elizabeth called out.

Anna poked her head in the door, then bustled through with a tray. Covered dishes, Elizabeth and Josef soon discovered, contained hot oatmeal, hot scrambled eggs, fat link sausages and creamy Czech kolaches, some with prune and others with poppy-seed filling.

"This will put the life back into you, Josef," Anna said proudly as she laid out the breakfast picnic-style on the bed.

Next she withdrew two jars from the large pocket of her worn button-up sweater. "Now these." She looked at Elizabeth. "This one in the brown bottle— he's to have three tablespoons now, three after dinner, and three at bedtime. He hates it and makes a fuss, but Anna knows best."

Elizabeth smiled. Anna spoke of Josef as if he were a little boy reluctant to take his medicine.

"And the one in the clear bottle is a ligament. You rub it on all his joints. Smells a bit like a hospital, but it works, doesn't it now?"

Josef smiled up at her. "My Anna."

"Now," she said. "I'll leave you two lovebirds to breakfast."

After she left, Elizabeth fed Josef his medicine, then they ate breakfast. Afterward, she rubbed the ointment on his aching parts. She stared down at his penis, playfully. "And do you need some here?"

"I think that's been taken care of very generously in other ways, ma'am."

They spent the day in bed, snuggling and kissing and touching each other, occasionally dozing. At one point, Elizabeth pulled a few vampire books from the shelves and read. Day turned to night—and as always—the wolves howled.

"They always seem so near," she remarked. "It's as if they are on a campaign of terror."

"They know who I am and where I live. They know this is sacred ground and it fills them with rage. Plus, I burn hawthorn wood in the fireplace, and roots in the cast-iron stove in here."

"It burns hot—fiercely hot," she said. From that single stove, the room could get quite warm.

"I know. The scientific name *Crataegus* comes from the Greek *kratos* meaning strong, which makes it perfect for stakes and arrows. But it also makes excellent fuel. It's the hottest wood fire known, which makes it ideal for heating the cottage—and better yet, the smoke drives the wolves mad."

As if on cue, the wolves howled.

"What do you think that means, when they howl?"

"In the wild, it's how they communicate. Amongst the vampires, I think it's a locator call."

Elizabeth shivered slightly and nestled closer to him. "I'm glad I'm here. With you."

Later, after gentle lovemaking, after she heard Josef's rhythmic breathing, Elizabeth lay awake listening to the creatures. She was afraid to sleep. Afraid to see through her twin's eyes in some twisted nightmare. Afraid that when she finally found David—because she knew Josef would make sure they did—that she would have to use a hawthorn stake to free her beloved brother from whatever state of undead he was in.

Chapter 12

Thwuck!

Standing near the cottage, Josef watched as Elizabeth shot an arrow at the target on the fence by the far side of the inn. After fifteen attempts, she finally hit it perfectly.

"Not bad," he said.

"Thanks. But I'm going to have to do a lot better than that. Consistently." She trudged off to retrieve her arrows, and he marveled at her. In the cold air, her cheeks were rosy red and healthy-looking. She had cut off the tops of a pair of her wool gloves to better grip the bow. Her long black hair was tucked up under a black woolen cap she borrowed from him, and she wore jeans and an Icelandic sweater.

He still felt weak—his bones ached, especially his spine—yet the sight of her warmed him. She was so utterly unexpected in his life. He had his hunt, and the recovery from each hunt. He had his papers and research and solitude. He meditated. He ate with Anna and Zoltan when the mood struck him. And he had long ago stopped wishing for that which he assumed he would never have: a woman to love and maybe even grow old with. She had been brought to him under the most tragic of circumstances in her own life. Wasn't that sometimes how fate worked?

She returned to his side and got ready to aim again.

"Steady," he said calmly. "Take your shot."

She released the arrow, and this time it was only maybe inches from its target. She immediately placed another arrow in the arrow rest, lining it up with the nocking point he showed her.

"Draw the string fully back to your face and use

the top of your hand to feel for a comfortable position…. The string should be just in front of your eye so you can look directly down the arrow shaft. You can do it, Elizabeth."

She aimed and found her target. Josef leaned over and kissed the top of her head. "A born archer."

She looked up at him, eyes shining. "You think so? You think I can do this?"

"I'm less than thrilled by what we're facing, love, but you have uncanny aim."

She practiced all afternoon, until he finally ordered her to stop. "Look at your fingers. They're blistered. You have to develop calluses. I doubt you'll be able to in the time we have, but turning your fingertips into a bloody mess won't help us."

He looked up at the sky. "Nightfall is almost here. Tonight, we'll study maps and talk about a plan. You realize that in order to reach the lair of the black wolf, of my biological father, we're going to have to sleep in the woods. No way around it. We can't hike it in one day. The trail is easier to find with the trees barren, but the snow will bog us down. It will be cold and wet and fairly miserable."

She gave him a pretend glare. "You're not talking me out of this."

"I didn't figure I would."

"What if they find us in the woods?"

"We fight to our dying breath. The general idea, though, would be to keep them from finding us. Or else to set up traps around our camp to give us an advantage."

Elizabeth slung her bow over her back. It was a large bow, nearly as tall as she was.

"I'm afraid of the dark," she said quietly. "Out there." She looked toward the woods and the mountains that crowded close to the inn's grounds.

Josef immediately thought of the darkness in the trunk where his mother hid him. "I used to be terrified of the dark. I told you about my mother hiding me. It was pitch black, hot and I could hear everything happening. I have nightmares reliving that night."

She wrapped an arm around his waist as they walked to the cottage.

"When I was a teenager, I still hadn't slept without the light on. One day, I had confided to a friend— my only friend—that I was afraid of the dark. He opened his mouth to some of his buddies, and they jumped me at school and threw me in a janitor's closet with the lightbulb removed, locking me in."

"Oh, my God, how awful."

They reached the cottage, stamped their feet to shake off the snow, and entered. Josef walked to the fire and threw on some more hawthorn branches. He stoked the flames.

"It was terrifying, positively terrifying. Eventually, the janitor found me, a mess, screaming to be let out. I ran home and told my father I would never go to school again. Ever. And he couldn't make me, I told him."

"What did he say?"

Josef pulled a bottle of brandy from his cupboard and two snifters.

"He said he'd been thinking about it. My problem. My fear of the dark. And Dad said, 'Josef, it finally dawned on me it's not the dark you're afraid of.'"

"Well, of course it was." Elizabeth looked at him quizzically.

"No. He told me I was afraid of what *comes* with the dark. Whether it's vampires or wolves… or serial killers. It's the *things* that go bump in the night. Not the night itself."

He handed her a brandy.

"Thanks," she murmured. "This should get rid of the chill…. Going back to the fear of the dark, your father sounds terribly clever. Did that help you?" She sipped at her brandy.

"Totally. From that day on, I made peace with the night, even so far as to find it beautiful, and decided I would figure out a way to combat the things that go bump in the night. At first, I planned on being a police detective, like Dad. But then as we solidified our theory on vampires and my birthright, I knew I was destined for this. Whatever sort of strange existence this is."

The two of them spent the rest of the evening poring over maps of the mountains. Much of it was just depicted as topographic shades of brown and tan and green, but Josef had also made his own maps, adding details and trail marks, landmarks of boulders and rock formations, and other notations to his depictions.

"Memorize as much of this as possible," he said.

"If for some reason we get separated, you're to try to get back to the inn here—" he pointed "—as quickly as possible. Don't stop for anything. I'll meet you back here."

"We can't get separated," Elizabeth replied. She rubbed his arm as she stared down at the maps. She sat at the table, sipping brandy and poring over the pages until the fire lost its glowing embers and the room cooled.

Josef went into the bedroom to toss some hawthorn roots into the stove, and to turn down the sheets and light a kerosene lantern. When he came out to the table, she was fast asleep.

He walked over to the table and sat down opposite her. Her face looked luminous by the glow of the two candles on the table. He only had electricity for a couple of hours each day by generator. She knocked the breath out of him. Seeing her felt like a kick in the gut—in a strangely good way.

He stretched out his hand and touched her hair, marveling at its softness. She had the tiniest scar, like a small white star, near the corner of her eye, and he wondered how she got it—a playground

accident? He smiled. He wanted to know everything about her. He stroked the small scar, wishing
he had been there that day—whenever it was—to
kiss it. He stood and went to the alcove to his makeshift altar. He knelt and spoke to both his mothers,
silently, in his mind.

*If you have sent her to me, then please keep
Elizabeth and me safe, and help me to destroy the
ultimate evil.*

Chapter 13

Elizabeth remembered reading maps, and then nothing. She woke up near dawn, allowing her eyes to adjust to the darkness. Josef was wrapped around her, the six or seven inches of his height advantage making her like the caterpillar in its chrysalis as he spooned her completely.

She managed to wriggle out of his arms without waking him. She rolled over to look at his face. When he slept, she saw part of that little boy in the police file. His face was wrinkleless, smooth. His curls gave him an impish, youthful appearance, even if his eyes were mature and haunted. But while he slept, eyes shut, that haunted look was replaced by a serene one.

She stroked his face, and then maneuvered closer to him, trying to preserve their peaceful slumber there in their warm, soft bed, knowing once they were hunting for the vampire clan, all would be dangerous and dark and ugly. Not to mention cold. They couldn't stay in their private cocoon forever.

It was still dark out when she heard a pounding on the cottage door. Josef bolted awake, wildly looking around. He grabbed her. "What was that?"

"The door." She pointed.

The two of them got up, each pulling on a robe. Josef peered out the window near the door. Mara was pacing impatiently and now barking.

"Can you see who it is?"

He shook his head, grabbed his dagger from the wall, then put his shoulder to the door. "Who's there?"

"Zoltan," came the shout from the other side.

Josef threw the door open wide. "What's wrong?"

He put the dagger down and ran his hands over his face and then through his hair.

"Fire!"

Josef stepped out on the stone entrance to his cottage. Elizabeth crowded near him. The icy air took her breath away, and made her doubly aware of the cold floor and her bare feet.

The three of them stared at the old barn on the other side of the inn.

"Call the fire department," Elizabeth urged.

"None to call," said Zoltan. "We're too isolated. We will have to let it burn."

"Do you think…?" Her question seemed to hang there, between them all.

Josef nodded. "Vampires are terrified of fire, but in their undead form, their human body, they're capable of setting them. Can't think it's anything but them. It's a warning. A threat."

"I thought they wouldn't come on holy ground."

"That part's not sacred," Josef explained. "It belonged to the caretaker, the original one, according to the Mother Superior's diary. He kept a few cows and a vegetable garden until he was killed. I

think that land was never part of the original conse-
crated grounds."

"Or they may be getting bolder," Zoltan offered.

The three of them stared as the flames licked the
pre-dawn sky. As shades of orange and pink spread
across the morning sky, traveling from the mountains,
the fire burned orange and red. It was, Elizabeth
mused, a rather awesome sight. It would have been
almost beautiful had it not been an obvious threat.

She and Josef went into the sleeping alcove and
dressed in warm clothes while Zoltan waited for them.
When they were alone, Josef whispered, "This isn't
good. They could be trying to lure us out into the
open. Worse, trying to get to Zoltan and Anna."

"Not sweet Zoltan and Anna. They're so harmless."

"Exactly. We're a liability here, Elizabeth. We're
going to have to cut short our training and take our
chances finding the lair ourselves."

Elizabeth bit the inside of her cheek. Her old life,
college professor, academic, was rapidly falling
away. This was all so insane. She thought of trying
to get word back to her department chair—but what
could she even say?

The two of them ran for the door. Then, with Zoltan, they raced across the grounds, occasionally slipping on ice, to the gate on the other side of the inn. They pushed through to the small, snow-covered garden patch, and then to the old wooden barn, now halfway to the ground. Acrid smoke involutarily tightened Elizabeth's throat. Her eyes stung. Bits of ash fluttered through the air, looking almost like snow flurries.

"Here," Zoltan said, handing her a white handkerchief.

She put it up to her mouth and nose to breathe through. It helped, but her eyes openly wept.

Josef coughed as he moved in close to the blaze. It seemed to singe Elizabeth's lashes. She couldn't imagine how hot the flames were to him.

"Oh, Christ!" he uttered, staggering backward.

"What?" Elizabeth called out to him.

He tried to shield her, turning around to face her and blocking her view.

"Don't treat me like a child," she said. "What?"

He shook his head. "Don't look, Elizabeth." He wrapped his arms around her in a fiearce embrace.

But Elizabeth wriggled and pushed against him. "No!"

Finally she saw his face relent. He pointed. Hanging from a beam in the barn was a body, charred beyond all facial recognition. Hung with wire, so it wouldn't immediately fall during the fire. Hung, so they would find it.

The body of a woman.

Elizabeth suddenly doubled over, clutching her temple. Zoltan put his hand on the small of her spine. "What is it, Elizabeth?"

"My head." She tried to stand and found she was wildly dizzy. The pain was sharp, like an ice pick, stabbing her in the temple. And then it came. In a flash in her mind.

It was the body of the woman that David had been forced to drink from. Elizabeth saw two vampires, hoisting her as if she weighed nothing, over the beam. The vampires were gaunt and very pale, their veins casting a bluish hue over their skin. She saw them tying the wire to the young woman's throat. They doused the body with gasoline. Then laughed like hyenas as they lit it. Elizabeth felt her heartbeat, pounding fast, like a rabbit's. She felt panic as she couldn't stop the scene from playing out in her mind. She squeezed her eyes shut and shook her head from side to side, trying to stop the vision.

The hanging body stirred.

Elizabeth opened her eyes and looked up at it. She saw it there, in the flames. Dead. Totally dead. But in her mind, it stirred. It flinched. Then she realized the vampires had let their victim live, just barely, only to put her through a final agony.

Elizabeth stumbled away, her head violently throbbing, bile burning the back of her throat.

"The sadistic bastards," she gasped, falling to her knees. "She was alive when they hung her."

Josef came over to her and knelt down in the snow. "Stick with it."

"What?" She clutched at her chest, feeling as if she couldn't breathe.

"Stick with the vision. Stick with it. What do you see?"

She grabbed her head and squeezed her eyes tightly shut again—but that did nothing to make the horrific vision stop.

"Two vampires, their eyes are…flat. Like dull black rocks. They're looking for you, Josef. Taunting you. Waiting for you."

"Can you see their lair? Can you see David?"

"He's…oh, now I see it. They brought him here. They're talking to him now. He knows I'm at the inn. He feels desperate. And there's the black wolf. Sleeping. He's enormous."

"What's around the lair?"

"Bones." She shook her head from side to side, and her teeth chattered. "It's so damp. I can hear the dripping water. And there are bloodstains all over the walls."

"Is it a cave?"

"No. It's underground, but made of…large stones carved into bricks. Gray stones, in some spots, but black in others."

She collapsed to the snow, grateful the icy wetness brought her back to the present rather than in her mind. "I can't see anymore. It's useless."

"No, it's not," Josef said. "Your vision showed us it's a ruin of a castle, or some ancient fortress. That will help us, because I think I know where we're going to search first."

Zoltan asked, "Do you want me to get Anna?"

"No," Josef said. "We don't want her to see this. We'll let it burn itself out, then bury the body."

"The ground's frozen," Zoltan argued.

"There's not much left to the body at this point. We can bury it in a pile of ash and leaves and let nature take its course until the thaw in spring."

Josef helped Elizabeth up. Her legs felt wobbly. The two of them started back toward the cottage. Zoltan remained behind to oversee the burning barn to make sure it didn't spread. Elizabeth looked back to see Zoltan's devastated expression.

"Are they safe here?" she asked Josef. "Would the vampires come on sacred ground?"

"I would have said no before. But now I'm not so sure. The inn is solid stone. They would have to go inside it to burn it down—and I don't see that happening. But if they formed pyres all around it, it's possible they could smoke them out."

"Why the escalation?"

"You. The seer. They've despised me for a long time, but now the ante is upped."

Back in the cottage, Josef paced. He looked over at her. "Please let me do this alone, Elizabeth."

She shook her head. "I can't."

"I've been preparing for this since my birth. Since the night my father stole my mother from me."

"My brother's with them. You…and he…are all I really have. Do you honestly think I could, if things went wrong, watch you be killed by them? While seeing it from afar? Watch it and be powerless to stop it? That frightens me far more than tracking them to a lair in the forest."

He kicked at a log next to the fireplace. "Damn them! Fine. We're going to need more weapons. Hawthorn arrows are deadly, but they only allow me to shoot one arrow at a time."

"How else can you kill them?"

"Lure them into the sun…trap them somehow. Fire. Hawthorn stakes or arrows. Stake through the heart."

"If they sleep by day, couldn't we burn them in their lair while they're in their coffins?"

"This clan doesn't sleep in coffins."

"Where do they sleep?"

"In caves, in ruins. Underground. The tubes in London, my father was convinced, were a veritable haven for vampires. Dark, dirty. They like being those things that go bump in the night. They need to be protected, to feel safe. Paranoia rules their world. They're more clever and cunning than you can imagine."

"Do they still feel human emotions?"

"You're a comparative religion professor. What are the various versions of hell of the major world religions?"

"Lakes of fire and all the rest of it."

"Right. But also, don't some define it as separation from God? Eternally."

"Yes. There are some interpretations that look at it that way."

"Well, vampires are as separated from their God, from their souls, as you can get. They have a strange jealousy and curiosity about human emotions, but most of them can no longer recall or conjure true emotions. Their thirst is for one thing. Blood. Liquid life. It overwhelms anything else in their existence. And that breeds a paranoia, a hatred for human souls."

"Can we attack them as they sleep in the ruins?"

He nodded. "But they may post guards. And we're going to have to bring kerosene or other fire-starters if we try that."

"What about some kind of Molotov cocktail?"

"Yeah. I better get busy rustling up ingredients. Their lair shouldn't be more than a two-day hike. We'll have Anna call into town to see if there's a weather report for the region. We don't want to get stuck in a blizzard."

He came over to her and kissed her forehead. "Scared?"

"Yes."

"Me, too. But we can't endanger Zoltan and Anna. We need to go."

"I know."

She watched as he left the cottage in search of items to make homemade Molotov cocktails. Alone, Elizabeth shut her eyes and tried to think of David. Her David, healthy and laughing, not some hollow-eyed minion of an undead master.

Even more scary...if they burned the lair, how would she free David without killing him, too?

Worse, who would she find? Her brother? Or some half-turned thing?

She didn't want to think about it. Then she had a horrific thought. What if David was seeing through *her?* She saw through his eyes, he through hers. Maybe she was telegraphing their plan to the clan. If so, she and Josef would walk right into a trap.

Chapter 14

Josef couldn't sleep. He stared at the ceiling and contemplated sneaking away and going to the lair alone. Every bit of his being wanted to protect her, wanted to keep her safe. However, with Elizabeth being a seer, he had no doubt she would try to find him. He imagined her either wolf bait…or freezing to death up in the mountains. He knew she'd never just let him go alone.

He sighed. He knew she offered some tactical advantage as a seer—but he felt bringing her would only weaken his position. No matter how it went down, he would do anything to spare her, and that meant the undead had an advantage, an edge they didn't have as recently as his last hunt.

He rolled over and stared into the darkness. He had filled some bottles with kerosene. He had also fashioned some of his bows with rags around the tips so he could dip them in kerosene, light them and let loose the fires of hell. However, he would have felt a lot better if his father was there.

Josef squeezed his eyes shut. The memory of the night when his father was captured ranked with his mother's murder as the most torturous of his life. The two of them had been at a ski resort near Harrachov. They had heard of a suspicious death, a skier found mutilated on the slopes. Whispers and murmurs were of a serial killer, but the local police, no doubt conscious of the effect on tourism, blamed wild animals.

"What do you think." His father scanned the peaks. "It's getting dark. We should head down."

Josef nodded and slapped his hands against his

arms to try to warm himself. "Do you have any more of that coffee?"

His father pulled his black wool ski cap down over his ears and shook his head. "We finished it after lunch. But I do have a flask of brandy." He grinned at Josef.

"Now that sounds inviting." He moved closer to his father. Then they heard the first howl in the distance.

"Christ," his father said. "We need to get to the lodge. We've waited too long to begin our descent."

Josef looked up at the rising moon. "We were so caught up in following that trail of blood. I think we're getting closer to their hiding spot."

"Well, if we don't watch out, we will indeed get closer—and not in the way we want. Come on."

They turned together and started down the mountains, their snowshoes helping them stay atop the heavy snow. Josef trudged as fast as he could, feeling his muscles burning from exertion, and knowing his father—though in excellent physical shape—had to be feeling it far worse at sixty-three years of age.

The night air was frigid, and his rapid breathing was making his face damp. Mentally, he urged himself on. Then he heard a howl close by. It almost sounded as if it were on his shoulder.

His father turned around. They didn't need to say anything to each other. Doubling their efforts, they plunged down the mountain, at times tumbling and falling as they moved faster. Snarling and growling sounds emanated from the trees around them.

"I think they have us surrounded, Josef." His father's voice was resigned.

"Then we fight to the death," Josef said, cursing himself for not seeing encroaching darkness and for following the blood trail so deep into the mountains. Perhaps it had all been a trap. Could the vampires be so clever?

They stood, backs to each other, and took out their arrows and bows. They prepared to fight as the first two wolves emerged from the trees. Josef was startled by their size—huge beasts with broad chests that looked ferocious. Josef shot at one—and missed. He loaded another arrow into the nocking point, shot again and landed an arrow in the wolf's side. It yelped, reared up on two legs, then turned, more fierce and frenzied than before.

"Christ, Dad…" Josef muttered.

"I know" was his father's breathless reply.

While Josef was preparing another arrow, two human-looking vampires emerged from the woods. The wolves seemed to retreat slightly, their growling becoming more subdued.

Josef, his back still to his father, said, "What do you think this means?"

"Nothing good."

The vampires were on the two of them in an instant. Josef thought he blinked and they were thirty feet from them, opened his eyes and they were inches from them.

The two vampires seized his father, who yelled and clawed at them, trying to reach for his knife. Josef wheeled around and pulled out his dagger, but one of the vampires shot out an arm and snapped Josef's wrist in the flick of a second. Pain radiated up his arm and through his shoulder and he stifled a scream.

He reached out for his father, but they were dragging him astonishingly quickly through the snow, as if his father—six-feet-two and a sturdy two hundred pounds—weighed nothing.

"Dad!" Josef yelled out. He started after them, but soon was surrounded by six wolves. They lunged at him, and he pulled out his dagger. His left arm was virtually useless, but adrenaline coursed through him and he drew up his dagger to one wolf as it rose on its hind legs. He slashed its throat and blood sprayed in a wide swath, spurting on him in a sickly warm gush.

As soon as the wolf fell to the ground, Josef took his dagger and pierced its heart. One of the other wolves attacked him, its teeth piercing Josef's arm, then again on his shoulder. He sliced at the wolf's head, nearly taking off its ear. It yelped and backed away, and then, with the other surviving wolves, retreated completely, bounding off after his father and the vampires.

Josef, losing blood from the two deep bites— puncture wounds from the fangs—started after them, screaming, "Dad, Dad!" until he was completely hoarse. He couldn't see their trail, though at some point in the night he heard his father's voice, in a final yell, echoing throughout the valley Josef now found himself in.

Exhausted, he droppped to his knees and fell into

the snow. He felt his own blood, warm and sticky, on his face. It mingled with ice and snow in a strange collision of senses. Lying there, he felt pain everywhere in his body. And then sometime in the night, unconciousness, blessedly, came to him.

The next day, two skiers had discovered him and taken him to a doctor. As soon as he was coherent, he checked himself out. By then, a vicious storm had blown in, obliterating any tracks in the mountains. Josef had turned back, tried again the next morning, and eventually, days later, gave up on finding his father.

He had never forgiven himself.

Josef sat up. The cottage had been a haven. Grief was always on him, like an ever-present companion. His soul had never quite healed, but the cottage was home. And this could very well be the last time he ever saw it.

He looked at the beautiful woman sharing his bed. Could they possibly hope for a future together or would that be tempting the angry fates, tempting the darkness itself?

Elizabeth stirred. "Josef?" she said dreamily, her voice husky. "You need to rest."

"I can't," he whispered.

She slid her hand to his thigh, tracing up with her fingers until she found him, hard and ready for her, despite his mood.

"Mmm, darling," she purred. "Come lie next to me."

He spooned her again, kissing the back of her neck, nibbling her, and making goose bumps rise.

"When this is all over, will you come to America with me and make love to me every night until we are both very old?" she asked breathily.

He moved his mouth next to her ear, pulling her even closer toward himself. "Keep thinking we have a future beyond these mountains," he whispered. "I have to think that, I have to believe it."

"Believe it," she said firmly into the darkness.

He maneuvered his body so he could slide into her velvet walls. As close to heaven as he guessed he'd find on earth. He rocked against her, reaching a hand around to touch her, then played with her nipples. He heard her breathing grow faster, more shallow. It amazed him how in sync they were. They both came at once. Then she wriggled around to face him, nuzzling his neck. The release made him drowsy. He kissed her, then felt himself relaxing and going to sleep, a curtain of darkness descending quickly.

Hours later, he awoke to the smell of coffee. He sat up. Elizabeth had set the table.

"Anna brought us her kolaches. She was crying, but pretending not to be…. You're the son they never had, you know."

He nodded. He felt his throat tighten. He waited a second or two, then said quietly, "I've never understood all the pain in my life. Cursed to be a dhampir. And yet, Zoltan and Anna…you…I have been touched by goodness. My father. My mothers—both of them. It's as if my life is some epic of a warrior of old, you know?"

She looked at him solemnly. "Anna asked me if you want her and Zoltan to care for Mara, or will she come with us?"

"No, I'd rather she stay here. I don't want to risk the wolves attacking her."

Elizabeth knelt down by Mara's side and

scratched between her ears. "She is so soulful, don't you think? You never said how you got her."

"I had shot a wolf on the mountain. As a dhampir, I can see vampires beneath the wolf's clothing so to speak. I see them where they are. Shadows that are really beasts. I had Mara in my sights, but I looked in her eyes and knew, she was an old wolf, a crone. A sweet half-breed. I put out my hand with some beef jerky as enticement. She came to me, and has been by my side nearly constantly since."

Elizabeth stood, walked over to the breakfast table, and sat down. He went and sat opposite her. He looked directly into her eerie pale eyes. They were resolute, but sad. Exactly how he felt. No words were necessary.

After breakfast, they dressed in long underwear and turtlenecks, layers of warm clothes. Then they dejectedly packed their heavy backpacks, took their bows and daggers, and opened the door. Josef took a last look around.

"We'll be back," Elizabeth said confidently.

"Wait one minute," he said. He put down his backpack and went to the altar in the sleeping alcove.

He took the photo of his mother, and then made the sign of the cross. He returned to Elizabeth, opened his backpack and placed the photo in it. "I just feel better having it with me."

She nodded solemnly, and they both left the cottage. Josef gently shut the door behind them. Then with Mara trotting beside them, they walked up to the inn. Elizabeth craned her neck and gazed up at the gargoyles.

"When I first arrived here, this place seemed ominous. Now it seems like a haven."

"It is," he said, taking her hand.

Anna was already a blubbering mess when they arrived at the front door and set their packs down in the entry hall.

"Be careful, you two," she said, clutching Elizabeth to her heavy breasts and smashing her against her housecoat. Zoltan kept clearing his throat, and Josef could tell he was trying to avoid a scene.

"Be careful," Zoltan said, voice quavering.

"We will," Josef said. He inured himself, bracing for good-bye, perhaps permanently. "Mara's food is in the bin by the front door. I feed her around five

each night. I let her out three or four times a day—
she generally stays in the field between the inn and
the cottage."

"We'll take care of her," Zoltan said, stopping to
pet Mara. But suddenly the she-wolf bolted out the
front door.

"Mara!" Josef called out. "Mara! Stop!"

Elizabeth cooed to the wolf, "Mara, sweetie,
come back."

But she was gone in a flash.

Josef felt his spirits deflate like the fog settling on
the mountain. His she-wolf was gone. This didn't
bode well for their quest at all.

Chapter 15

Elizabeth put her bow into the backseat of the rather rusty old car they were taking, and covered it with a blanket. Their plans included driving on a narrow mountain road to a village—or what passed for one up in the mountains: an inn, a few houses and a small general store.

The car had belonged to Zoltan's brother at one time, and they were ostensibly borrowing it, though none of them knew, as Josef and Elizabeth left, if the car—and its occupants—would ever return.

The late-model Renault shuddered and groaned with each gear shift, which gave Elizabeth and Josef the giggles and broke up the tension. It was a ridiculous little car, and Josef was way too tall for the front seat, driving with his knees practically hitting the steering wheel.

"This reminds me of a clown car in the circus," Elizabeth said, laughing.

"I'm so glad my poor knees getting whacked with each turn of the steering wheel amuses you." He grinned slyly.

The Renault let them know when it resented the climb higher in the mountains.

"I think it has altitude sickness," Elizabeth teased.

"Very funny." He rolled his eyes. "It's all fun and games until the vampires come."

"Don't remind me."

"Listen, when we get to the inn, remember what I told you."

She nodded. "Trust no one. In the mountains, anyone can be one of their spies."

"We're simply honeymooners, backpacking in the mountains, and then headed for some skiing."

"It amazes me the tourism business here."

"Less expensive than going to the Alps and just as majestic, in my opinion. But where we're going, the villages fall away. Some of it is national park. There are ruins, and rock formations, even a place that looks a bit like Stonehenge."

Elizabeth felt a flash of heat sear through her brain. She touched her temple.

"What?" Josef asked.

"Nothing. I just…I don't know. Something about when you mentioned the rock formation."

He glanced over at her. "You all right?"

She nodded. "It was just a flash. A split-second."

"Okay," he said. "Maybe shut your eyes and rest." He resumed concentrating on the narrow road.

Elizabeth stayed silent. She found the drive dizzying. If she looked out her window, the drop at times was precipitous. She prayed Josef's driving skills would allow them to arrive at their first stop safely.

About fifteen minutes later, Josef suddenly slammed on the brakes. The car skidded, and one wheel slid off the road.

Elizabeth shrieked as the car leaned. She grabbed onto her door handle and held on.

In the road, a mangy wolf stood, head low, snapping its jaws, growling.

"It's a vampire."

"What do we do?"

No sooner had Elizabeth asked the question that the wolf leaped onto a rock, and then disappeared into the forest. Meanwhile, their car still perched dangerously.

"Hold still. Stay calm," he said. "Slowly open your door."

Elizabeth did as he instructed her. Inching her way, she climbed out onto the road. When she was safe, he, too, opened his door. The car shifted, and Elizabeth tried not to scream. The Renault was such a rustbucket, she barely knew where to try to hold onto it.

Josef emerged from the car, and together they rocked it back and forth in an effort to get all four tires back on the road. "On three," he said.

Using all her might, muscles aching, she pushed. Gravel crunched and trickled over the edge and down the ravine. But after several tries, they got the car back on the road. Both of them hopped back in to continue their journey.

"When I saw the wolf, I braked, and I think I skidded on a patch of black ice."

"What do you think that wolf means?" Elizabeth asked.

"I've learned in the way that I can see them, they can detect me—and you. It's not good that we were spotted. No doubt the beast is howling a warning of some sort."

They drove on for another two hours until they reached the small village where they planned to stay the night. In the morning, they would take a trail deeper into the national forest. They couldn't chance questions about their bows and arrows, so at the inn, Josef locked the car carefully, blanket over the bows, and they donned their backpacks and walked into the inn, for all the world like two lovers on holiday.

Josef spoke fluent Slovak. Elizabeth had a skill for language, and picked up a few words here or there. The gist of it was the innkeeper had a room, and if the two of them wanted supper, the dining room was open.

Josef took the key the desk clerk handed them.

Then the clerk asked Josef another question. He nodded and responded. Then, taking Elizabeth's hand, Josef led her up the steep wooden staircase to the second floor where their room was at the end of a dark narrow hallway. Once inside, she unloaded her pack.

"What did he ask you?" she whispered.

"What we planned to do up here in the mountains. I told him ski and hike. I said we were married at Christmastime."

She looked at him, feeling a surge. How she wished that was true. Marriage, a normal life. She wanted her twin brother to meet Josef—really meet him. David as his real, loving self. She imagined them all at her dining room table, laughing over jokes, discussing philosophy and religion, drinking wine from one of the Virginia wineries she'd discovered, their experiences here fading into memory.

"I hope you don't mind, Elizabeth. Pretending that."

She shook her head.

"In my heart, I feel like we are bonded."

"Me, too," she said quietly.

They washed up in the hall bathroom, then changed into fresh clothes for dinner. In their packs, they had some sort of K rations bought by Josef when he last traveled to Prague. Dried beef jerky, bread from Anna, hard cheeses, dried fruits and other portable food items completed their supplies. Josef had told her he could kill birds—plentiful in the mountains—or deer or rabbits if need be. They both hoped that their journey into the mountains wouldn't last longer than their food supply. In any case, they descended the main staircase of the inn, determined to fill their bellies at the last home-cooked meal of any sort for a little while.

In the dining room—about ten tables and a long bar staffed by a barkeep and one waitress—only one other table dined. The four men sitting at it, rough and grizzled looking, stared at them suspiciously when they walked in. The ceiling was probably twenty feet high, cavernous, yet made of a dark wood that set a gloomy, oppresive mood. No music was piped in, and every whisper seemed to reverberate off the walls.

The waitress, a thin, pinched woman with graying hair and dull brown eyes, recited the menu—all various dumplings and stews. Elizabeth wondered how anyone in the Czech Republic kept their weight down with so many rich, plump dumplings at nearly every meal.

The other men had their heads bowed, talking in deep but subdued voices. Night fell, and the view outside the window to their left grew midnight black. Elizabeth thought that nights in the mountain were going to be terrifying indeed unless the moon was full.

Their supper arrived on plain, dented pewter plates, and they ate in near-silence—so different from their meals and conversations back at the cottage. Elizabeth missed Zoltan and Anna—and Anna's lovingly prepared kolaches.

About a half-hour later, when they were ready to order a cup of tea and pay their bill, two men strode in and immediately looked directly at them.

Josef muttered under his breath, a half-whisper, "Vampires."

Elizabeth looked at him. "You're sure?"

He nodded.

Elizabeth turned her head slightly and watched the two men as they walked over to the bar. She was horrified but immensely curious. They were both very pale, their skin almost luminescent. In fact, one of them had veins on his forehead that pulsed an eerie blue.

Their voices were flat, lacking any animation or emotive quality at all. Even though they were speaking Slovak, and she could only glean a word or two, the flatness spoke volumes about their humanity.

The dining room was illuminated by two hanging chandeliers with beeswax candles, and several sconces on the walls. Even in the dim lighting, Elizabeth could see the vampires' eyes might as well have belonged to a corpse. They were dull like worn stones.

The barkeep served the undead two lagers. When they brought their beers to their lips, Elizabeth, watching surreptitiously, saw their fangs, pointed and long.

"Can we go?" she asked Josef. She struggled to find her inner courage.

He nodded. The waitress brought their bill. He left the correct amount of Czech crowns or *korumas,* plus a tip, and they stood. Immediately, the vampires turned their heads and flashed malicious smiles, the points of their fangs giving their faces an animalistic angularness.

Elizabeth instinctively took Josef's hand, and they left the dining room and hurried back to their own room. When they were alone, she begged him to leave the inn.

"I'd rather be out in the night than cornered here."

"We can't. We have no camp, which means we've laid no traps. We're better off battening down in here, maybe even taking turns keeping watch."

She knew what he said was reasonable, but her instinct was to run far away. He was a hunter, she was an academic. She supposed it was rather like fire-fighters trained to run *into* burning buildings while the rest of the world would run out. She wanted to leave this place with every fiber of her being, but she had to train herself to be more like Josef. To think like a hunter.

Their room on the second floor had a single narrow curtainless window, with a very long drop to the ground below. They made sure the window was locked. After, they deadbolted their door, and Josef placed a chair wedged under the doorknob as extra security.

"Trust me, this isn't enough to keep them out if

they're determined." He opened his backpack and took out a crucifix. Then he took out a vial.

"What's that?"

"Tincture of hawthorn. I also have hawthorn berry oil. The scent should drive them off, or at least weaken them or make them uncomfortable."

He took the tincture and drizzled it across the floor, in a line. Then he took it, drenched his finger in it, and made the sign of the cross on the door.

"Do you believe in Christ?" Elizabeth asked him.

"Hmm?"

"You made the sign of the cross. Do you believe in its power?"

He faced her. "When I was a young man, my physical pain and agony, the loss of my mother, then my adoptive mother... I stopped believing. Wouldn't you?"

"I might," she said softly.

"I became an agnostic. But my father was a man of great faith. And I saw him take courage when facing the serial killers we hunted, when seeing the worst the world could display. We faced down vampires, and still his faith was unmoved. It was his rock and fortress, and salvation. *A mighty fortress is our God,* as the old hymn goes. So I reexamined my faith. And now, it does give me courage. I have right on my side. Light. Good. They have the devil, darkness, evil. The classic battle, as old as Christ and Satan in the desert itself."

For some reason, the sight of him making the sign of the cross on the wooden door made her feel a little better. She undressed and put on one of his flannel shirts to go to sleep in.

"Coming to bed?" she asked, standing on tiptoe and kissing his cheek, then kissing his ear, gently blowing in it.

He groaned softly. "I wish this place was the cottage. You know how to turn me on."

"The same could be said for you," she whispered as his hands moved down to the small of her back and then lower, to the curve of her spine and then her ass.

They stood, kissing each other deeply. She pulled back, looked up at him, then she laid her head against his shoulder.

And then she saw them.

"Josef!"

He turned his head in the direction of the window, where she pointed, mouth agape. Two glowing eyes amidst an eerily pale face seemed to be suspended in the night.

"Shit," he muttered. He opened his backpack and pulled out his dagger.

"Don't open the window!"

At the same time they were staring at the face reflected in their window, they heard a scratching at their door.

"I'll stay here by the window," Josef told her. "You go get more hawthorn oil and soak a towel with it, and stuff it against the door, on the floor."

Elizabeth pulled a bath towel from the top of the dresser, doused it with hawthorn oil, and pushed it up against the crack under the door. The scratching grew more intense, then she heard something scurrying away—something large, with a thumping like it was dragging something larger along with it.

"God, it sounds like a giant rat," she said, finding herself shaking. "I have the creeps."

"The one at the window disappeared."

"So now what? It's not like I can sleep." Her heart was palpitating.

"Let's try to get some rest. We can do two-hour watches. You sleep first."

"I couldn't."

"You have to try."

Elizabeth lay down. The bed was hard and lumpy, and the blanket was a scratchy wool one. Josef came and sat down on the edge of the bed. He took his hand—masculine and strong—and stroked her forehead. "I will never tire of looking at you."

She rolled onto her side and stared up at him. "I feel like my entire life has been…in one dimension. And now, like a fog lifting in the morning, I see things how they really are, with the darkness and vampires all around."

"Think of a good memory. Tell me a happy story about you and David."

She smiled. "There are so many. Like a lot of twins, we were the best of friends, even during those pre-adolescent years when girls think boys have cooties and vice versa. I remember once, it was after our mother had died. We were in sixth grade, I think. A boy I liked had said something horrible to me. He said I was so flat chested I was concave—and proceeded to snap my training bra in front of the entire class."

Josef gave her a lascivious look. "If he could see you now."

"Hmm. Well..." She smiled up at him. "David gave him a black eye—and got a bloody nose for his trouble. Then, that night, he and I sat together and watched an old movie on television. Our mother loved old movies, and we used to watch them to sort of feel close to her even though she was no longer with us. And in the middle of the movie, David looked over at me, all serious, and declared, 'Lizzie, I've decided. We're going to go to college together. That way I can always protect you if any boy is mean to you ever again.' Even all those years ago, I found that so sweet, so chivalrous. And...we did. Went to Harvard together."

"Lizzie? Is that what he called you?"

She nodded. "Still does."

"You don't seem like a Lizzie to me. You're too

sophisticated, too beautiful. I think of Lizzie Borden when I hear that."

She laughed. Then she heard a thumping on the roof.

"Did you hear that?"

He nodded. "They're above us. In the attic, maybe."

"What about the inn's owners? The barkeep? Don't they hear all this?"

"I told you, this place is likely a hotbed for their spies. We're like Daniel, descending into the lion's den."

The ceiling above them started thumping louder and louder. "Christ!" Elizabeth said. "So much for sleeping."

The noise continued, along with hissing, high-pitched keening and guttural cries, until nearly dawn. The two of them tried to shut it out. They ended up lying down with the dagger beneath their pillow, and talked.

Near dawn, the noise stopped.

"They need to get back to their lair," Josef said, yawning. "We should sleep a couple of hours."

And at that, the two of them fell asleep, within minutes of each other. Elizabeth, as she shut her eyes, said one simple prayer. *Please, Lord, just one request tonight...no dreams.*

Chapter 16

Josef could read trails better than the most experienced park guides. His father had taught him to read a compass when he was a little boy, and his adoptive mother was an amateur astronomer. It was nearly impossible to see stars over the bright lights of London, but on holiday, she would show him the night sky and point out Ursa Major and Draco and Cassiopeia. Those lessons of hers had helped him all these years later, and he wondered if her love of stars had been almost fated.

He and Elizabeth had sipped rich cups of hot chocolate that next morning and had eaten kolaches—not nearly as good as Anna's. They bought boxed lunches for the "hike," and bade the innkeeper farewell.

Next, they had climbed into their rust bucket and drove a short way up the road. They left the car in a pull-off area meant for vehicles to have a turnaround spot on the narrow roads. Then they hiked back down the road a ways to a trail—a different trail from the one at the turnaround, the better, they hoped, to deflect anyone following them.

Josef had no idea if his schemes and plans would result in anything but the delay of the inevitable, but damn, he'd try.

They took their bows, slung them across their backs, and entered the trail. It was narrow and marked by yellow triangles. Josef's plan was to hike to a Stonehenge-like structure the first night, and sleep sheltered by its stones.

Elizabeth had assured him of her strength. She said she hiked the Blue Ridge frequently—but the Blue Ridge's peaks were not the height and altitude of these mountains. In addition, though she told him she frequently weathered the cold on these trips, the overnight temps and dampness from hiking in snow would hinder them. Frostbite was a real possibility, but then again, so were vampires.

Josef took the lead, his stride long. He kept looking over his shoulder, making sure she was keeping up. Their ascent was steep, and he kept his eye on the peak. The hike was too strenuous for conversation, so he remained focused, though lost occasionally in thought. It was difficult not to think of his father on the mountainside.

Around midday, they took a break. Josef lit a small fire and melted snow until the water boiled. Gratefully, they each filled a tin cup with hot tea.

Elizabeth shuddered. "Just what I needed. A little heat to warm me up inside and out…. How are your joints?"

"Honestly? Not bad. I think I'm so keyed up about what we're facing that I'm not focused on my pain. I won't lie to you. I ache, but I'm managing."

He pulled the box lunches out of his pack. They ate two hearty rye and beef sandwiches, accompanied by their tea, and each drank water from their canteens.

Josef looked up at the sky. "Sundown will be here

in maybe four hours. We've got to move along if we're going to settle in for the night."

"How far beyond that to the lair?"

"If it's where I think it is, from your visions, I'd say another full day's hike, closer to the border of Poland."

She nodded and stood, stretching her arms upward.

"Sore?"

"A little," she admitted. "But last night's vampire rats, or whatever noise they were making, didn't help much."

"Well, I don't know how much sleep we're going to get out here."

"I know. Cold, wet and on the lookout for vampires."

They threw snow on their fire, causing smoke and steam to sizzle, hoisted their packs and started up the trail. They passed two male hikers, giving a curt nod. Then they continued on.

After two hours, they could see the Stonehenge-like formation. Six rock piles were assembled in a semicircle. The rocks were immense, and Josef knew they were on a natural plateau with a flat rock creating a centerpiece. Josef's strides grew faster. He was anxious to set up camp, secure it as best as possible, prepare for battle if need be.

The stones dwarfed them both. But nothing, Josef decided, had prepared him for what they found.

She stared. "That's not…"

"I'm afraid it is."

The stones rose in oddly shaped pillars. Four or five huge boulders with flat edges were stacked one on top of the other. Josef knelt down on the rock. He ran his finger along the granite. "Blood."

Elizabeth's face registered devastation. "It's where human sacrifices have been offered!"

"Appears so. And this is fresh." He pointed to a damp spot of rock.

Elizabeth put her hand against a rock, looking like she needed to support herself, perhaps feeling weak-kneed at the thought of victims meeting their end there, an executioner's graveyard. As soon as she touched the rock, he saw that she had a vision.

"Oh God, David was here!" She took her hand from the boulder and drew back.

Josef came to her side and gently but firmly put her hand back on the stone. "Stay with it."

He watched her face contort into one of pain. He hated to push her to see what happened at the site, but they needed to know what they were up against.

She shut her eyes and bit her lip, then exhaled. "No wolves," she said. "Human form. They brought a…child here. Sick bastards! It's a little boy. A small boy like you. There's a tall man…he's absolutely ruthless. He walks up to David and pushes him down on the rock next to the boy. He hands David a dagger—it looks ancient. He orders David to kill the boy and eat his heart. David refuses, but I…can tell he's getting weaker. His head is pounding. The tall man is very strong. He lifts up the boy with one hand…by the throat. It's like the boy is a rag doll. He…bites him. The boy doesn't struggle. He's sick. But…his body is shaking. The man tosses the boy down…now the other vampires are feeding on his tiny body. There's blood on the rocks, and one of them even goes so far as to lick the rocks. The noises are horrible, and David is covering his ears."

She fell to her knees. "It's over now."

Josef glanced up at the darkening sky. "We don't have time to find a defensible spot in the woods. We're going to have to stay here."

"That would be like staying at the site of slaughter. This is unholy ground, as opposite of the inn as one can imagine. We would never be safe here."

"I know, but we're safe nowhere until dawn. We can set up a hiding spot for ourselves there." He pointed to the crevice between two boulders.

"It's narrow."

"Yes, but hidden." Josef planned to essentially boobytrap the entire stone tablet. "You go, set up a sleeping spot, unpack food, and then help me. I'm going to gather firewood. We'll set up kerosene-dosed pyres all around us. If we come under attack, I have fail-safe matches—they'll light even if wet. I'll light some of my kerosene-tipped arrows. Fires will greet them, which will terrify and confuse them, then we'll use our bows to kill as many of them as possible."

Elizabeth looked around. "Josef…"

He heard the doubt in her voice. This place *was* unholy ground. But they were in no position to leave it. "Trust me!" he demanded. "I don't have time to tell you that this is the *only* plan we have for tonight. If you don't want to die tonight, then you need to do what I say!"

Elizabeth lifted her chin. Her bottom lip quivered. But in the end, she gave a single nod and went to prepare the crevice.

Josef immediately set to work. He grabbed kindling and firewood and established pyres at strategic defense points. He had enough kerosene for this night, to lay a trap at the lair, and maybe two extra nights. After that, they would not have fire accelerants. Like any commando, he had to get in, get out, get safe. His entire plan depended on getting to the lair tomorrow and leaving it in the night, all the vampires destroyed, David safe. In other words, the impossible.

Sweat formed on his brow, and he could tell with the aching in his bones that it was going to be a cold and bitter night. They had each other to keep warm, but dawn and the sun couldn't come soon enough.

Elizabeth emerged from the crevice, still looking upset with him. She was foraging for firewood nearby, and he went over to her.

"I'm sorry. I didn't mean to be so abrupt."

"It's all right. Circumstances don't get much worse than this."

"No, I suppose they don't."

She turned her back to him and continued searching for precious wood. Occasionally, he saw her shoulders shake—with emotion, not cold. He felt worse than ever. Bringing her had been a mistake. Leaving her behind wouldn't have been that much better.

When all the pyres were ready, they retreated to the crevice. The moon had already risen; a half moon, but extensive cloud coverage blocked it from view.

In the crevice, they lit a single small candle, and nestled against each other. She had laid out a simple dinner—hard cheese, dark rye, dried apricots and some protein in the form of beef jerky.

"A feast for a king," he said. "Or at least a man in love." He reached over, put his hand on her face, and drew her to him. Kissing her lips, he said, "I will not let us fail."

They ate in silence. Josef stared up from the crevice. The sky was pitch black, though occasionally the clouds would part and the glimmer of the moon would shine down on them.

And then they heard it. The first howl.

Her fingers gripped his arm.

"We have a plan, and we'll stick to it," he said calmly with a confidence he didn't feel. He had set down a path of kerosene to their hiding spot, which he could light, and then pull his bow. "They first must find us."

"I feel like prey, sitting here, waiting for them."

Josef was used to the hunt. Had she not been with him, he would have gone into the woods, stalking them, always on the move. The howling increased, growing on all sides.

"How many do you think there are?" she asked.

"Five." He had gotten used to discerning the subtle variations in wolves' calls and howls. His own dhampiric senses gave him uncanny abilities of sight and hearing.

"How many are in this clan?" Elizabeth asked.

"It's been impossible to determine. For every one I slay, more take their places."

She wrapped up the rest of their half-eaten dinner and put it in their packs. She lifted her bow, took an arrow, arranged her weapons. He glanced at her.

"I will feel better if I'm ready."

He smiled at her. "So will I."

He checked his weapons. "You cold?"

"Not anymore. Amazing how nerves will do that to you."

They heard the wolf to their left first. Paws on stone.

Josef put his hand on her shoulder and gave her a hand motion that told her to wait. Wait. Patience. He knew better than to reveal their position for a single wolf. Better to have the element of surprise. She cupped her hand around the candle, shielding its light.

Next, to their right. They heard a different growl.

Still wait. Josef imagined that Elizabeth could telepathically read his mind. Perhaps it wasn't so crazy to think that way. They were intuitively connected.

The clouds parted, and they were able to see each other's faces. He mouthed the words, "On three."

She nodded.

He crouched, and so did she. They readied their bows.

They heard growling behind them, then the paws padding on stone in front of them. Josef held up one finger. Then two. Then three.

He lit the accelerant with the candle, which invoked flames from their crevice to the first pyre.

He lit his arrow and fired with perfect aim at another pyre.

The wolves reacted with ferocity. Yelping, howling, snarling. The sounds were spine chilling.

Josef could see in his peripheral vision that Elizabeth landed an arrow perfectly in the side of one of the wolves. That was his girl!

He struck another pyre, then another. Acrid smoke traveled heavenward and choked the stone formation, and flames licked the sky.

The wolf Elizabeth struck was yelping and on its side. Josef aimed for the last pyre, standing, bow poised, when a wolf leapt from behind and bit his arm.

Elizabeth screamed, as Josef pulled his hunting knife from its sheath and slit the wolf's throat. Then, when it fell limp to the crevice floor, he pierced its heart. When his blade penetrated the heart wall, the transformation began. The process was always sickening as the wolf coat disintegrated into clumps of hair and blood and intestinal filth, revealing a corpse beneath it. This one was female, her features pale, her skull draped with shriveled skin.

Four more vampires to go.

Josef decided they had to come out of the crevice in order to gain a shooting advantage. "Let's climb out on the stone. You shoot to the right, I'll go left."

"I'm with you!"

Again, in unison, they emerged. She landed an excellent shot, and he hit a wolf with a kerosene-tipped arrow. It exploded in a blaze of fire.

"Get them with fire," he yelled at Elizabeth. "They turn to ash."

They lit their arrows in the line of flames running from their crevice. Around them, the pyres blazed. Smoke burned his throat, and he hit a wolf in its hindquarters. Again, it exploded into a fireball. Had he known this would happen, he would have been fighting them with kerosene all along.

The pyres continued blazing. Two wolves were left. The wolves kept circling, their heads down, ears perked up, snapping their jaws.

"Their eyes glow red," Elizabeth said.

"I'll take the gray one, you take the one with the black and brown fur."

They lit their arrows, and the animals went crazy. Elizabeth's wolf, rather than retreating, came leaping for her, knocking her to the rock below them. Josef released his arrow, hit his wolf, which burst into flames, then used his fist to beat the wolf now pinning Elizabeth to the ground. He knocked the wolf off of her as she punched at its snout. The wolf yelped at the assault, but as soon as it rolled over and landed on its paws, it leaped, snapping at Elizabeth again and missing her face by inches

Josef grabbed his hunting knife and pierced the wolf's side, but it turned at the last minute, taking the knife with it, which protruded, not entering the chest cavity.

Elizabeth scrambled up and grabbed the end of a fiery bough, bringing the flame down on the wolf's head as it turned to bite her. The blow knocked it down, and at that point, Josef twisted the knife. The body transformed to vampire, dead. Cold. Pale. Covered in excrement and black blood.

Elizabeth collapsed on the stone, looking at the destruction around them.

"Vampires, zero. Us…five."

"I know," he said, squatting down. "Which doesn't bode well for sneaking up on the lair tomorrow."

"Well, I wasn't expecting an engraved invitation."

He smiled, his first release from tension all evening. "Come on," he said. "Let's try to get some rest. Let the fires burn out."

He held out his hand to help her to her feet, and they retreated to their stone hiding spot. It was covered in blood and wolf hair. Gathering their things, they moved to one of the stone pillars. They spread their sleeping bags out, but chose to sleep in a single bag close to each other, trying to keep warm, trying to keep the nightmares at bay.

Josef knew, within a few hours' hike were the ruins of the old castle he guessed was the lair. When the sun rose, they would have a day to get there and set their trap. Like a man facing an executioner, he knew they'd either live free or die. Twenty-four hours.

Finally…he would stand face-to-face with the man who sired him. The man who murdered his mother. The man he despised.

Chapter 17

Snow fell in thick flakes. Elizabeth awoke with the pale sky above her, and wet, heavy flakes landing on her cheeks.

"Josef…" She nudged him.

He groaned. He looked faint, and she knew this entire ordeal had to be taking its toll on him. She longed to have him in America, safe, resting. The University of Virginia had an excellent medical college, and she hoped one day they might be able to help him.

Josef stirred and rubbed his eyes like a little boy awakening from his nap. Then he startled fully awake.

"Snow," she said, giggling slightly.

"Of course," he moaned. "Because we need snow to complicate matters."

Elizabeth rose and stretched. The stench of charred flesh and the smoky ashes of the pyres were all around her. Gray ash mixed with snowflakes, giving the world around them an eerie appearance. In the safety of daylight, she felt comfortable starting a cooking fire, and went in search of fresh kindling. As she walked, she passed wolf carcasses; mostly ash. She would be glad to leave these unholy rocks.

Returning to Josef, she lit a very small cooking fire while he carefully took inventory of their packs.

"We're okay on the kerosene and food. But we've got to get to the lair today."

Elizabeth leaned over the fire, warming her hands, and trying desperately to shield the flames from the increasingly heavy snow. It was of no use. The snow fell faster, and at an angle, dousing the burgeoning fire, which soon extinguished with a hissing sound and steam.

"No warm breakfast today, I'm afraid." She stood and shrugged, but she couldn't recall a time when she felt colder than right now.

"Here." He held out a small metal object, square, but with rounded edges.

"What is it?"

"You light it like this." He flicked it like an old-fashioned lighter, the kind her grandfather once had. "Then you close it, and voila! A hand warmer."

She took it, and curled her hands around it. "Heavenly," she murmured.

"That will burn for eight, maybe ten hours. You can put it in your pocket, or wrap your hands around it. I sometimes put them in this." He showed her an elastic belt. "It holds it against your body. If you put it on your back, it will warm you all the way through."

"Thanks." She looked skyward, and snowflakes immediately clung to her eyelashes.

"We better get going. No telling what this snowstorm holds."

They started trudging through the snow, setting their sights on the peak of the mountain. From there, Josef was certain they would have a view as far away as the Hawthorn Inn, and possibly the lair itself, which he was certain stood carved into a mountainside.

Within fifteen minutes, Elizabeth's jeans were soaked, and she had to walk virtually bent over into the wind. Her legs stung, as if they were getting small electric shocks. She was grateful for the handwarmer; it was the only thing warm on her entire body.

She walked in Josef's footsteps, and she could tell his stride was slowing and growing smaller. The cold and wetness had to be agony for him.

A while later, Elizabeth looked down. The snow, which had been ankle high when they left, was now mid-calf. It was falling at an alarming rate. She wrapped her scarf tighter around her face, covering her mouth, feeling herself sweating with the exertion.

About an hour later, they finally reached the summit. The wind howled, in contrast to the eerie silence of a heavy snowfall, muffling all noise.

Josef lowered his pack and his bow, and dug out a pair of binoculars. He scanned the landscape. He spotted the location of the lair and handed her the binoculars and pointed. "There."

Sure enough, through swirling snow, she spied the castle ruins built on the side of a mountain. Crumbled, covered in moss and foreboding, it would take every ounce of strength and speed to get anywhere close to it before nightfall.

"If we don't make it there tonight—" she exhaled "—where will we sleep?"

He took the binoculars back. He pointed. "Over there, in the east. Looks like a grove of cedar trees. We might be able to hunker down there."

He continued looking through his binoculars and then turned completely around. "Oh, my God, Elizabeth!" He handed her the binoculars, and she peered through them.

"Oh, no." She covered her mouth with her hand.

There, in the far, far distance, was clearly the smoke of a fire. It snaked up into the sky.

"By my compass," he said, looking down, "that's the inn, or close to it."

"They have to be fine," Elizabeth said resolutely. "They just *have* to be." She squeezed her eyes shut, trying not to let her mind wander to the tiniest thought of Zoltan and Anna being hurt.

"We need to go. No time to grieve, no time to rest. Just revenge. That is our focus."

"Revenge…and David."

He nodded at her, and they grimly started the final leg of their journey. As they walked down the other slope, they both slipped and slid. Elizabeth landed on her ass several times, and on one occasion smashed into a tree.

"You all right?" Josef asked, coming to help her up.

She nodded, fighting tears. Everywhere she looked, there was only falling snow. She felt as if she was being driven mad by white.

"At what point—" her teeth chattered "—do we call this a blizzard?"

"Let's aim for the cedar grove. It's no use trying to go farther than that. The good thing is this storm may keep them inside, and it will obscure our tracks. The bad news, of course, is no fire, no real shelter…and they'll be extra bloodthirsty tomorrow night."

Elizabeth felt a depressive gloom descending over her. Mentally, she thought, *If we make it until tomorrow night.* But to Josef, she merely said, "That sounds like a good plan. We need to get into dry clothes."

By the time they reached the cedar grove, Elizabeth could barely do more than shuffle her feet. Their situation was dire. If the vampires didn't get them, frostbite would.

In the thick of trees, they were protected, slightly, from the wind, and Elizabeth could actually blink normally, instead of with clumps of snow and ice sticking to her lashes. But for both of them, shivering was out of control and made even the smallest movements difficult. Elizabeth's hands felt swollen. Her numb fingers made her clumsy.

Josef had packed a small hand shovel, and he dug down to the hard ground in a natural shelter of trees. Opening his pack, he placed a waterproof tarp on the exposed earth.

"Our sleeping bags are waterproof. If we zip them into one, pull another tarp over our heads, and let nature and the snow take their course, we'll actually be warm."

She managed to smile wryly at him. "Sure we will be." Her teeth chattered.

Lighting a fire was hopeless. So she listened to his directions, and piled branches on top of the second tarp, which in turn covered their sleeping bags. With the falling snow, it wasn't long before they were, indeed, quite hidden.

"We'll climb into the sleeping bag, and once we're in there, strip naked," he said. "Get out of these wet clothes."

"Are you out of your mind, Josef? It's twenty degrees and a blizzard out and you want me to be nude?"

"I'd like you nude all the time, Elizabeth." He grinned at her. "But really, our body heat will keep us warm."

So, feeling as if she was climbing into her own tomb, she wriggled down into the sleeping bag. Soon, he was in next to her, and they both wrestled with their wet clothing to get undressed. Her legs were chapped raw and red, and she felt like she was going to freeze to death. When he put his body next to hers, all she felt was *his* cold and damp skin.

"Hungry?" he asked her.

"Not really."

He reached behind him and got a canteen and apricots. "Well, at least drink something. Getting dehydrated won't help us. You have to force yourself. Eat a little bit, too."

She drank some water, but her stomach was clenching so much from the cold that eating made her feel ill. She'd wait until they warmed up a little.

"What do you want for Christmas?" Josef asked her.

"Christmas?"

"I just want to talk and get our minds off the fact that we're in a blizzard on a mountaintop with no hope of rescue should things grow worse."

"Christmas was *over* a couple of weeks ago."

"I know, and I missed it, so *this* Christmas I'll have to get you something extra special."

"Oh, well then diamonds are a girl's best friend," she joked.

"Yes. But hot coffee is a girl in a blizzard's best friend."

"Actually, I think my best friend is growing suspiciously friendly," she teased, pushing her ass back against him.

He laughed, kissing the back of her head. "It's so quiet, isn't it? Almost peaceful."

She listened. The snow muffled everything. The

sky had grown very dark, and in some ways it was terrifying. In others, it was as if it were just the two of them in the entire universe.

They lay there like that, until, if Elizabeth was to guess, it was ten o'clock. After a time, he was right; she felt warm. Not toasty, but not shivering. She ate some apricots, drank some water. And blessedly, she heard no wolves. The wind rustled the cedar trees. Occasionally clumps of snow fell on their sleeping bags, which actually just made them warmer.

She heard Josef breathing heavily. Elizabeth rolled onto her back. The blizzard had stopped, or at least slowed. She stared up through the cluster of cedar trees and could spy sky and stars. A cedar cathedral for her to worship the beauty of nature and appreciate for just this moment that she was alive.

She brushed a tear from her face. The blizzard only delayed the inevitable. Tomorrow, they would have to reach the lair or turn back.

"Hold on, David," she whispered. "Just a little longer."

Chapter 18

She awoke to the sound of Josef retching.

"What can I do?" she asked and put her hand on his back.

"Kill me and put me out of my misery!" he snarled.

"You can't mean that," she scolded.

"Can't I? My birth has been a curse." Again, he retched, and she winced for his pain.

They were both still naked in their sleeping cocoon, though he had pushed back the tarp and fresh, cold air assaulted their senses. The day was crisp. Clear.

Josef collapsed back on the sleeping bag. "I'm sorry."

"I understand. But we've got to move, Josef."

"I know. Get dressed and leave me for a moment."

She didn't argue with him, knowing how he did not like being seen in his weakness. She fished through her pack for a fresh set of clothes. She donned long underwear, a new pair of jeans, and two pairs of wool socks. Her boots were still wet and putting them on was agony.

"Finish the apricots and the bread," Josef told her. "Take your boots off and use the plastic bags to wrap around your socks as a layer from the dampness of the boots."

She did as he suggested and was soon completely dressed. She decided to give Josef his privacy and walked out of the cedar grove and looked up at the next peak. Above the treeline, there was little cover for them. Lichen and shrubs dotted the peaks, but the trees tapered off. It seemed as if geography would afford them few hiding spots from this point forward. Their best hope was finding the stone formations, or else staying low to the ground.

She thought about Josef's plaintive cry. To wake every morning in the face of unbearable pain took a courage and fortitude she could barely imagine.

"Okay, beautiful," he said, limping up behind her, comical in long johns and boots but not clothes. "I'm over my little exercise in self-pity. Time to face the beasts."

She whirled around and hugged him. "Whatever happens, I will never abandon you."

"We need to talk about that, actually."

"Why?"

"If I am caught, just leave. Make your way to the road, and from there try to get to Prague. Go to the American Embassy and weave a tale of serial killers up here. Perhaps that will get some real police working in these mountains."

"No. I won't leave these mountains without you and David."

"You see my pain. I'm a liability right now. But I know this, if I die on this mountain, I won't consider that I would have lived in vain. But if I thought that *you* would have died here, too, then it would be too much."

"Well, sorry…" she said firmly. "Put some clothes on. We're going."

She turned abruptly and went to pack up. She sensed he was standing stock still, not moving. She glanced over her shoulder. "Yes?"

"Nothing. I just adore you. You're unbelievably stubborn, but I adore you."

They were hiking by eight. The sun wasn't really shining but was covered in a foggy kind of aura. However, at least it wasn't snowing.

The day passed uneventfully, however, as they hiked beyond the treeline, and into more barren, though still powder-covered, areas.

He spoke over his shoulder. "We'll also have to watch for bear—though they should be hibernating. And there are lynx and wild mountain cats up here."

"Wonderful." They were prey for vampires, and now they were somewhere along the food chain for wild animals.

Elizabeth followed Josef carefully, trying to keep her steps in his. Her thighs and calves ached because every step involved lifting her legs high to pull her feet out of the snow and move along.

She trudged behind him, and they stopped for lunch shortly after one.

"How are we doing on time?" she asked, pulling her hat down over her ears.

"Not good. We want to be there." He pointed. "On the ridge, when dusk falls. Then I plan on setting my traps. When they're all—or most of them—sleeping in the morning, we'll go in."

With no map of the inside of the castle ruins, no idea how many of the enemy there were, tiredness, cold and snow, Elizabeth knew the odds were ridiculously skewed against them. They made a small cooking fire, warmed up with tea, hurriedly ate hard cheese and a k ration each, and packed up and continued their desolate journey. As dusk descended rapidly, they were within striking distance of the castle ruins. It barely resembled a castle anymore. A turret jutted up toward the sky, but it was mostly crumbled stones hewn into the mountains.

"Now what?" she asked as they stood gazing at it.

"There's a stone formation there." He gestured with his hand. "We'll hide until it's dark and then plan an assault. Let's get our pyres ready. You go that way… I'll head this way, and we'll meet back here in twenty minutes."

She looked up at his face. His five o'clock shadow had progressed to a rough beard. She kissed his cheek, and rubbed her hand on his stubble. "Very handsome, love." She smiled at him. "See you in twenty, then."

He turned away and waved to her, and she went to gather kindling, then logs. She was rushing along, moving quickly to stave off her chill, looking for dry wood, when she heard them. Not wolves…but human keening.

Out of nowhere they came, swooping down, pouncing on her so quickly she hadn't time to react.

She thought there were four of them. Men of uncommon strength who could lift her as if she were a cat's toy in their paws. Their voices reminded her of fingernails scratching down a blackboard. Their sounds were inhuman. No horror film director had ever or could ever duplicate their demonic chorus.

She screamed with pain and terror as the one with long black hair lifted her by the neck. He literally tossed her to another vampire, this one holding her by the hair and dragging her.

"Let me go!" she shrieked and tried not to panic, tried to ascertain where Josef was and if they had him, too. She was dragged along the ground as she kicked wildly, screaming until her throat hurt, snow landing in her mouth as her face scraped along the ground, twigs tangled in her hair.

She heard Josef calling for her. "Elizabeth, what's happened? Where are you?"

"Vampires! Over here!" she screamed. One of them, trotting along beside her, kicked her viciously in the gut. She couldn't breathe as all air left her lungs, and bile burned her throat. Her panic grew. She kept trying to take in air. She was certain she would suffocate to death. Then, finally, as the world started going black, her diaphragm relaxed slightly. She took in a tiny breath, but she still couldn't scream.

Now another vampire lifted her, dragging her nearly upright, her feet not even touching the ground. She tried to punch him, but he had her arms held tight to her body, his arm wrapped around her like a vise. Up close, he had an odor—she presumed it was of death, or rot. His skin was not as luminous or transparent as the vampires in the inn that she saw.

This one had rough skin covered in pustules. He made her want to vomit.

Then, suddenly they stopped. They were near a rock—a large one—and a member of the clan moved it as if it were a pebble. The vampire holding her ducked, then jumped down, and she realized she was being taken underground. The darkness was nearly total, though apparently the vampires could see just fine.

The one carrying her looked at her and smiled, his fangs showing maliciously. They were so pointed and looked as sharp as straight razors. His eyes were silver—as if they were made of liquid mercury. The tunnel was damp, dripping—as in her vision with David. The air made her retch and gag as it had the odor of rotting meat or worse.

They dragged her, and she heard rats scurrying, or other vampires. Her heart beat wildly. She told herself she wasn't afraid of the dark. She wasn't afraid of the dark. Just the things that go bump in the night. Unfortunately, though, the things that go bump in the night had now made her their prisoner.

Chapter 19

Josef heard her screams, and then nothing. Silence. He could see in the dark well—*that* he inherited from his biological father. He used to astonish his adoptive parents by spotting things from far off— even at night. It was a superhuman ability—but he still did not see as well as the undead.

From a distance, he could tell she was seized by them. A few of them, who wrapped around her like shadows. At the moment of her capture, he was digging at lichen to start a smoky fire. He heard her shriek, and immediately ran in her direction. When he got to where she had been, there was sign of a struggle, but she was not there.

He tried to fight the panicked terror he had for her safety, and instead channel it into cold fury. Running to their packs, he found their bows intact, along with the kerosene Molotov cocktails. He'd flush the devils out with fire.

Josef tracked them, trying to stay focused, but all he heard were her screams as she was dragged along the unforgiving ground. Josef swore he'd kill them with his bare hands, rip their undead hearts from their chests and light their corpses on fire.

The snow had drag marks, wide swaths of a path where she had been pulled along behind them. Josef knelt down and touched one spot, scooping snow and bringing it to his nose.

Blood.

They had hurt her.

He stood in the woods, trying to listen for them, but all he heard was the blood rushing through his own body, the pounding in his chest.

It had happened again. Ripped from him. Someone he loved. How could God do this to him?

Their tracks stopped at a stone. Josef looked all around, but no fresh pathway could be seen. He knelt down. Then he lay completely down in the snow and looked at the base of the stone. It had been rolled away. He was certain it was a tunnel— likely a path of defense for the castle's former inhabitants in times past. Now, it was a labyrinth of hell to the lair.

Josef leaned against the stone, to no avail. He didn't have their strength. There, they had the advantage. However, he knew from experience that blood lust interfered with their brains. They were easily upset by fire and would turn on each other with no concept of loyalty. Josef leaned against the stone and tried to formulate a plan.

Breathing hard, he realized he would have to go in through the main entrance to the ruins. If they captured him, he could hope to be brought where Elizabeth was and formulate an escape from there.

"Come on, Josef," he said aloud.

He tried to think like his adoptive father, who

combined instinct and methodical precision to any maneuver.

And he came up with a better plan.

Elizabeth, he spoke to her in his mind. *Stay alive. I'm coming for you.*

Elizabeth woke up in a sumptuous bed, certain she was dreaming. Ivory-colored silk sheets caressed her skin. The aroma of honeysuckle filled the air. Above her was a canopy. She was utterly bewildered.

She put her hand to her cheek. It was swollen, and her head hurt. Moving her fingers from her cheek to her scalp, she felt dried blood and an area where a chunk of hair had been ripped out by its roots.

She sat up, and her head pounded ferociously, like the worst migraine she had ever suffered. She breathed in and out evenly, waiting for the dizziness and pain to subside.

Slowly—ever so slowly—she turned her head and looked around the room she was in. Candles glimmered. The only clue she had that she was not someplace warm and truly safe were the walls, from which no amount of scrubbing could remove the patina of mold and flaking.

She looked over at a low table near a worn antique couch. On it rested a silver bowl filled with dried fruits and bread. Her stomach rumbled.

But she couldn't eat. Her mind was working overtime. She had no idea where she was or how she had been brought here. Her throat was parched and sore, but she was too frightened of being poisoned to drink from the decanter of water next to her bed.

She looked down at her hands, and then lifted a lock of her hair to her nose. It was damp and smelled fragrantly of rosewater, or lavender, perhaps. Someone had bathed her—or at the very least washed over the cuts and bruises she had suffered.

She struggled with her memory. She had been seized, dragged along through snow and against rock. Then the awful journey through the tunnel, then…nothing. It was as if she had fallen down the tunnel and lost all memory. Had she passed out?

She slid her legs over the side of the bed, placing her feet firmly on the floor. Not quite trusting her knees, she stood up cautiously and, while wobbly, was okay.

Her room was windowless. She went to the large

wooden door and found it bolted from the other side. She turned from the door and walked the entire perimeter of the room, every inch of wall, running her fingers along, looking for something, anything, that might be a clue or help in her escape.

She was standing looking at a painting of a woman in Gypsy garb when she heard a key turning in the lock, and the door groaned open on its hinges.

"Hello, Elizabeth," said the tall man standing there. He shut the door behind himself, but stood a respectful distance from her, hands clasped behind his back.

"Hello," she said, uncertainty in her voice. He looked very much like Josef, with a swarthy complexion and dark hair flowing to his shoulders.

"I was sorry to bring you here under such... forceful circumstances."

"Who are you?"

"That's not your concern right now."

"Where is my brother?"

"Soon enough. Soon enough."

"Josef...where is he?" she asked even as knots twisted in her gut.

"I expect, knowing how determined he is to bring this clan down, that he will be along shortly."

Elizabeth, in her mind, tried to warn Josef away. *Go...don't come for me. It will be a trap.*

She had no idea what time it was, what day it was, or how long she had been unconscious.

"Do I seem...uncouth to you?"

Elizabeth eyed the man. He looked so very much like Josef, only paler, and with a deadness in his eyes. He took two steps closer to her. The pupils were fixed. That was why he seemed so corpselike. If the eyes were the window of the soul, he had none.

"No man of manners would carry off a woman like that." Almost unconsciously, she touched the swollen part of her face.

"Tsk, tsk..." He reached out a hand to her face. "I'm sorry for the unfortunate manner in which you were handled. But I didn't think you would come here voluntarily."

"Of course, I wouldn't." His fingers were icy, and the skin's texture was unusual. Waxen. It caused an involuntary chill to pass up her spine. She looked him in his dead eyes. Could he feel any sympathy for her? "Can I please see my brother now?"

Her question was answered with a sneer. "I have a proposition."

"Which is?"

"Join me voluntarily, and I will free your brother. Fight me, and I will turn him."

"That's no choice. That's…suicide."

"No." He grabbed her in a tight embrace. "It's life. Eternal life. Freedom from death and suicide. Like your father. Did he solve anything by taking his own life? Do you really believe he joined your mother in eternity?"

Elizabeth swallowed hard. "Don't talk about them." She felt out of breath, weak.

"Had they but chosen my path, they would be together. Forever. Lifetime after lifetime. No sickness. No death."

Elizabeth shook her head. She hated what he was saying, hated the scent of honeysuckle, the mirage of luxury. It was all death. All of it. Death and evil. She longed for Josef. She wanted to see David.

"Let…me…go." Her voice was even. Firm.

"Last chance," he whispered. Suddenly, and without warning, he grabbed her hair. She winced at the renewed pain and saw stars in front of her eyes.

"Please," she begged. But any further pleas were cut off as he viciously covered her mouth with his, forcing his tongue between her teeth. She struggled, fighting against him, despite her aching muscles and weariness.

His lips were cold. They weren't like Josef's kissed in the snow. Josef's lips, despite the frigid air, were warm, his tongue pink and pulsing with blood. Josef's mouth was a haven, and she hungered for it. But this unnamed man's mouth was icy. His tongue felt like cold meat on a butcher's slab, and Elizabeth felt physically ill at his touch and at his kiss.

Suddenly, he withdrew, and pushed her hard, away from him and backward onto the ground.

"Now, my dear Elizabeth, with your revulsion so obvious...you have just sealed your fate. And your lover's, and your brother's."

She glared at him, but he only laughed.

"Remember, in your torment, you had the chance."

And with that, he turned around and left the room. She heard the key turning in the dead bolt, locking her in again. She was left in silence in the flickering candlelight. Left to think about her fate. And of the fate of the man she loved and the brother she adored.

Chapter 20

The day—or was it night—passed agonizingly slowly for Elizabeth. She felt like a caged canary waiting to be brought down into the coal mine to certain death.

Every time she shut her eyes, she envisioned the kiss of the mysterious vampire. She didn't want to—there was nothing pleasurable about it. But like a recurring nightmare, it replayed over and over in her mind. She tried to shut it out with other memories, positive ones—of Josef. They had come together for so brief a time, but everything about the experience was intense and full and passionate. She cared for him so much, and the thought of him coming to rescue her didn't stir any sense of hope in her. Rather, it reinforced her dread. How could they hope to overcome the desperate odds they faced?

Flashes of David filled her head. She saw him, smiling in the sun on Martha's Vineyard. And there he was in another memory, the time he dressed up as a girl for Halloween—she'd even curled his hair with a curling iron! But then, just as quickly as the beautiful flashes came to her mind, ugly visions of David with the vampires at the barn crowded them out.

Elizabeth clutched her head. She tried to promise herself that if they turned her, she would not forget her humanity and would rush out into the dawn and turn to ash. But could she hold on to her soul and humanity just through sheer will?

She didn't want to cry, but the tears welled anyway. Frightened tears. And then, as the first salty drops traced their way down her cheeks, again turned as she heard a key in the lock and the door swung open.

Only this time, it wasn't the mysterious vampire

who refused to give his name. This time, leering
vampires, bald, with veins pulsing along their skulls,
came in, slurping and licking their lips.

She was sitting on the floor, her head between
her knees, and she pushed herself backward, in an
almost crablike crawl, trying to delay the inevitable, delay them even *touching* her. But touch
her they did, grabbing her roughly, and with no
thought to her pain, pulling her out of the room and
into a dark hallway. She felt as if they would rip her
arms from their sockets, and she scrambled with
her feet to support herself somewhat. But it was of
little use.

In the tunnel, Elizabeth's screams echoed off the
walls. She felt as if she would lose her mind. Occasionally, her hand, or her cheek, would brush against
slime or greasy hair, a bone, or a moving thing…a
rat or worse.

After what seemed like miles of damp tunnels in
pitch darkness, she was hurled into a cell, smashing
into the far wall. The cell door slammed, and she was
left in darkness.

She tried to control her panic. *You're not afraid*

of the dark, she told herself. She heard breathing. Something was in there with her.

She curled herself into a tight ball, and tried to make herself as small and hard to find as possible.

The breathing grew a little louder. Then, a gutteral moan.

God, if they were going to kill her, just get it over with.

Then, she remembered her hand warmer. It had a faint glow, she remembered. She reached under her sweater and twisted the belt around, pulling out the warmer. It had a barely red glow, like the faintest flick of ash on a cigarette lit in darkness. She held it aloft. The cell was small, maybe eight by twelve. It was carved of solid rock and had a heavy wooden door with an iron grate in the center of it.

And against one wall, slumped, bruised, bloody, very pale and thin, sat David.

"Oh, my God! David!" A sob caught in her throat and she started trembling violently.

He lifted his head in the direction of her voice.

"Go away, demon. Don't mock me." His voice was weak, and cracked on the words.

"I'm not a demon, David. I'm your sister."

"You're a figment of my imagination."

He was losing his mind.

Not that she could blame him. How long would her own mental state last in here? She would soon be just like him—or worse.

Cautiously, to not alarm him, she moved across the floor in tiny steps, hands held in front of her, palms open in a gesture of peace. "It's me," she soothed.

When she was three or four feet from him, she squatted and held the hand warmer up to her face so he could see.

"It's me. I got your e-mail. I came to Prague. I came to look for you. And I was captured."

His eyes were flat, haunted, but they weren't liquid silver, which gave her hope they hadn't turned him. He was filthy, and she could see his hair had fallen out in patches. She felt her own scalp. There was fresh blood from where they'd dragged her.

He didn't register recognition. He sat there, dull-eyed, and seemed to stare through her.

She took another step closer.

"David…it's me."

"Get away!" He put his head down on his knees, and his shoulders shook.

Then she remembered something. "No…look."

Hurriedly, she pushed her hair off her face. Then she held the hand warmer up to her cheekbone. "Look. Remember when I got this?"

She had a small heart-shaped scar from when the two of them had been running with sparklers on the Fourth of July the year they turned seven. She fell down and the sparkler singed her there, and she had cried so hard that David wanted a matching scar, as if somehow that would make her feel better. He touched the sparkler with his hand. Sure enough, the sparkler had burned him, too. Then they'd both gone crying to their father. After that, whenever she was sad—a broken heart, a disappointment—he would take his palm and touch her scar with the matching one on his hand. Twins in every way.

At first, he didn't react. Then, she saw a single tear trickle down his face. He suddenly reached out to grab her and pulled her to him.

"Oh, my God, it is you," he whispered. "Oh, my God. What have I done? I've brought you into this mess. What have I done?" He sobbed, and leaned his head against hers.

"Shh, David. I'm okay. Shh…" She patted his face. "We're going to get out of here." She said it with a faith she didn't really have.

They sat in the darkness, holding fast to each other for a few minutes. Then, Elizabeth pulled away and sat next to him, close.

"Remember our language?" she asked him.

He smiled. "Of course."

"Well, let's use it so no spies can overhear us."

So, using the cadence and language long dormant in their adult lives, they began talking. The made-up "twin" language came back to both of them fairly quickly.

*Shakelpe, shandoke, modentay…*words Elizabeth thought she had forgotten, came rushing back. She felt a surge of happiness at using their private words.

After an hour, she had pieced together his story. He had come to Prague to see its sights and art. While there, he met someone who told him the Karkonosze mountains were as magnificent as the Alps. But one night, while at a pub, he ran into a rowdy bunch of rugby players from Germany, along with some hangers-on. At one point in the evening, someone had handed him a fresh pint of ale. He woke up two days later with no recollection of anything—and the worst case of the flu he had ever experienced. He'd been drugged.

The rugby players were gone. The hostel where he was staying was curiously empty. Even more odd, his wallet wasn't stolen, his cash and traveler's checks were undisturbed. His passport was where he'd left it in his backpack. The only item taken, as far as he could tell, was his photo of him and Elizabeth. The other reminder of the night of carousing was that flu.

Days disappeared down a black hole. Fever, hallucinations. For some reason, he felt drawn to the Hawthorn Inn. He heard of it while at the hostel, and like a siren, it called to him. He hitched his way there, barely coherent. No one in their right mind would pick up the American with the pale face, sweaty skin and sunken, dark-rimmed eyes. But he did manage to catch rides with farmers and rode with livestock, heeding this incessant call. To the inn. The one with the stained glass.

He stayed there, feverish and with the chills 24/7, but the scent of the hawthorn bushes—even dormant—made him sicker. He thought it was allergies. Then he thought he was simply succumbing to some sort of rural illness.

Driven to leave the Hawthorn Inn by the sight and scent of the trees and bushes there, he traveled onward, a wanderer. It never occurred to him to go back to Prague and civilization. To return to America or London. He was driven by some unseen force to go farther into the mountains, until he was captured.

Elizabeth had listened, heartsick, as he described his captivity. She told him about her visions, and he said his experiences were exactly what she saw. Unlike Elizabeth, who had Josef to explain to her the concept of dhampirism and vampirism, David had to grasp his experiences on his own. He knew something supernatural and evil was at work, but he was unable or unwilling to fully comprehend it.

"I don't know what to make of this place, these fiends," he whispered. "I thought they were part of a cult."

"A cult of immortality. A blood cult," Elizabeth said.

"How did I even end up here, Lizzie? I mean, you followed the thread to the Internet café in Prague—but then what?"

For her part, Elizabeth told David about Josef, about the affair—and how much deeper it was than that. And how, she hoped, at that moment, he was planning to rescue them.

She grabbed David's hand. "What do you know about this place? The ruins?"

"Not much. I've been in here most of the time except when they pull me out for some of their mind games."

She nodded.

"What about the leader?"

"They call him Lad."

"Lad?"

"Diminutive for Ladislav. He claims he was a Gypsy. A great leader of the Gypsies. He hates human beings. Hates the Nazis for exterminating his people and taking their possessions. And he's turned that hatred into a bloodlust. I thought he was delusional."

"There was a portrait of a beautiful Gypsy woman in the bedroom where he kept me. Maybe he once loved her."

"Any emotions, if he's really a vampire, are long gone."

"Except rage."

Elizabeth looked at her brother slightly illuminated by the slowing flickering hand warmer. He wasn't turned. That was the blessing. But now she wondered for what purpose they had been captured. Why did Lad want them—and want them alive…for now?

Chapter 21

At some point, Elizabeth and David fell asleep. She had rested her head on his shoulder, and he had slumped against her.

Whether they slept an hour or a day, she couldn't be certain, but soon, they were roughly roused by vampire guards. The fiends swung the door to the cell wide, and pulled Elizabeth and David up, flinging them into the hallway. Elizabeth had never been so viciously handled in her life. Their strength appeared effortless.

She reached out to grab David's hand, and she

was struck, hard, by one of them, who hissed. Another one growled like a rabid dog. Then, being pushed and shoved along the same disgusting corridors as she'd been dragged down before, she and David were taken to another room, this one as cavernous as their cell had been small.

It was a temple. A temple to Ladislav, to darkness, to the drinking of human blood. Along the wall were iron sconces with flickering candles. A large slab sat in the middle of the room, and on it, a woman lay, naked, tied like an animal with leather straps.

Around the prisoner were perhaps fifteen vampires. Some looked bored, some thirsty—licking their lips. And some simply murderous.

Elizabeth and David were pushed to the floor near the slab. She exchanged looks with the woman, who was gagged. Her eyes so clearly said *help me*. Elizabeth mouthed a simple "I am here," not even knowing if the woman understood English, but hoping her eyes conveyed compassion. Beyond that she could offer no help, no comfort other than her humanity. The woman would not die alone.

Elizabeth looked at David. To think he had witnessed this kind of torment over and over again in his captivity. And why were they brought here? Was it as Josef thought, that they were seers and thus a danger? Then why not kill them already? Turn them.

The room had an air of anticipation. Elizabeth silently prayed for the soul of the intended victim, and then for her own and David's souls. She couldn't bear the thought that either of them would be the last to go, would witness the death of their own twin.

She heard him first. His footsteps were crisp, powerful, strides of a confident man, a leader. Her captor. The cold, undead man who had kissed her.

He stood by the slab, arms raised. Ladislav, looking nearly identical, Elizabeth now realized, to his son, Josef.

"Ahh, Elizabeth…remember my words to you."

She sat, trembling.

"My family," he said to the room, to the undead. "I give you—" he gestured at the terrified woman on the slab "—life. Don't I always care for my family? Always provide for your every need?"

He knelt down beside the woman, and whispered. Elizabeth heard every word.

"Don't worry…death in this manner is excruciatingly painful. You will wish for death as they eat you, drink you, consume you. But only when they tap into this vein here—" he touched her thigh "—or the mother lode, here—" he touched her jugular "—will sweet death come. You'll wish for it. Wish and beg, like many, many, many women and children…and even men…before you. Then, when you're a corpse, they will have a party with you. They will rape your corpse and abuse it, until even your own father wouldn't recognize you. And then…nothing. You will join a hundred other corpses and rotting flesh, and no one will ever know what happened to you. Your family will have no peace. They will wander this world, perpetually grieving. So *know* that."

Elizabeth's eyes streamed tears freely. How could any person—no matter how long a vampire—lose all humanity?

Ladislav stood up on the slab. "Let me hear you, children," he screamed, his voice echoing.

The hissing was horrendous. Elizabeth likened it, again, to fingernails scraping along a blackboard. It was inhuman, and reverberated and echoed on the cavern walls, as if coming from a thousand directions.

"Feast!" he shouted.

At his command, the fifteen vampires fell upon the woman. Elizabeth went to put her fingers in her ears. But he came up behind her and pulled her arms straight upward until she thought he would rip them free of her body.

"No, listen to every sweet sound so you never forget it."

The sounds were as Josef described from his mother's murder. Hissing, keening and sickening slurping. The woman moaned and whimpered through her gag, punctuated by higher-pitched sounds that would have been shrieks were they not stifled. Elizabeth looked over at David, who she feared would vomit.

When they were done with their victim, one of them climbed on top of her and did just as Lad had promised.

And then, when the nightmare could get no worse, Elizabeth was lifted up off the floor.

"And now…guess who's next?" Ladislav said.

David screamed, "Nooooooo!" and stretched his arms to her.

One of the vampires strode over to him, black motorcycle boots echoing on the stone floor, and kicked David in the face. "Silence!"

David was struck unconscious, and Elizabeth was lifted up high, over their heads, again, as if she weighed nothing, and laid down on the now empty slab. The slab was slick with still-warm blood. Several of the vampires were licking the floor around her.

She tried to use her powers as a seer to reach Josef. *Don't come in here, darling. It will be death for all of us.*

Don't witness this.

It will kill you.

Josef felt Elizabeth's soul calling out to him. He was certain of it. She was alive, and that filled him with hope and fury.

"Elizabeth!" he shouted. But she was nowhere in the darkness on the mountain. Still, he was certain she was still alive, that she was trying to contact him, seer to dhampir, soul mate to soul mate.

But then he became concerned that time was running out. He couldn't wait until dawn for them to sleep. The time to act was *now*.

His pyres were set in the mountains surrounding the castle ruins. He hoped that perhaps the smoke might attract the attention of forest rangers. If that happened, they might send a helicopter or plane. If the fires looked deliberately set, the pilots then might send people to investigate.

But he could not rely on outside help, and he knew he would have no second chance. He wasn't going to leave any kerosene for the journey home because he didn't intend to leave any vampires alive. He knelt behind a stone, securing the Molotov cocktails to his belt. He treated the arrows with kerosene-soaked strips he tore from a T-shirt, wrapping them with precision.

It was time.

He lit a small kindling fire at his feet, cupping his hands to nurture the flames. He set an arrow into the nocking point on the bow, lowered the tip to the flames, stood, took aim and fired. It landed like an Olympian's arrow lighting the flame in the pyre.

The pyre ignited in a burst.

He aimed and shot four more arrows, each again landing with perfection. Then he hid behind his rock and waited.

Flames licked the sky, climbing higher, and better yet, the pyre near the entrance to the ruins billowed with smoke.

Josef heard them. Their shrieks reminded him of…he couldn't quite place it. The shrill cry of a hawk maybe, only harsher, higher-pitched. He saw dark figures in the turrets and looking out from a ledge in the ruins. They knew he was coming.

What he hoped, however, was that his path of pyres, the smoke and dancing flames, would make them afraid to exit the ruins through the front entrance, which would mean they might, of their own volition, leave via the tunnel, and conveniently move the boulder for him.

He crouched low now, not wanting to reveal his position. Sure enough, a boulder down near where Elizabeth was taken shifted. He saw three black-garbed figures emerge from behind and start running. They moved haphazardly, with no visible plan. That was typical, he had learned. They lacked thinking skills. Only the leader, he believed, had an astounding intellect.

Josef lit his arrow and fired on the vampires. The first one burst into flames with a shriek.

He lit a second arrow—and got the same result.

But the third vampire had seemingly disappeared. Josef wondered if there was a second underground entrance. From a defensive point of view, in centuries past when the castle must have been built, it would have made sense to have more than one underground tunnel in the event of an attack from one direction or another.

Josef lit an arrow and ran, low to the ground, to where the boulder was rolled away. The arrow was both illumination and weapon.

He leaped down, hitting the rock bottom with a jolt to his spine, causing him to wince. He looked down the corridor. What he saw revolted him.

Bones—femurs, arms, skulls—and rotted corpses, rats feasting on them, lined the floor. He had no time to react to the sights. The stench was overwhelming, and he was certain some of the odor was ammonia—bat guano. He steeled himself and charged up the corridor. A vampire stood maybe thirty feet down from him. He fired his blazing arrow, and the beast burst into flames.

With the heat from the flames singeing his eyelashes—the first time he'd felt warm in two days—he used the fiery corpse to light another arrow and continued his plan of attack. He lit up another corpse, passing it slumped against the wall, stepping on rats in full madness, running from the fire like leaving a sinking ship.

He fired another arrow and hit a female beast in her leg, and the flame traveled upward, engulfing her face and turning her to ash.

He paused to ignite a Molotov cocktail because he could see he was coming to a crossroads. He hurled the flaming bottle to his left, and a tremendous explosion occurred, followed by shrieking. Then he traveled to his right, running with purpose but essentially blindly. He had no idea where this maze would end. He knew labyrinths and cairns, like in Scillies, were circular in nature. Would all paths lead him to the center, to his biological father, the beast who murdered his mother? And where in this maze was Elizabeth?

He ran, trying to keep his bearings about him as the corridors filled with acrid smoke. Bat guano was igniting, and flames were spreading everywhere. He pulled a bandanna he had dampened in snow up over his mouth to breathe through. Again he came to a crossroads. He lit another firebomb, hurled it at a figure to the left of him, and at the precise moment he saw his target ignite and heard its shriek, something or someone hit him on the head with what felt like a large rock.

As the world turned dark, he called out her name. Someone leaned down close to his ear.

"Don't worry…we'll bring you to her." Then Josef was struck again and saw only blackness.

Chapter 22

Ladislav slit Elizabeth's sweater with a dagger.

"My son has excellent taste in women." He leered. Then he put his mouth down on her neck, letting the points of his fangs touch her—but not pierce her skin. "And I wonder," he said, as he drew away from her, "how it is she will taste."

He placed the dagger right beside her, though her arms and legs were tied so it was of no use. She kept moving her head to one side, trying to see David. He was breathing, and occasionally he moaned or stirred, but he was still lying down on one side, spittle forming in the corner of his mouth.

She looked up at Lad and tried to fight the panic. His eyes were liquid silver, the pupils fixed and devoid of any emotion besides anger and a thirst for power—and blood. She tried to mentally brace herself. The pain would be finite, not infinite. It would *feel* infinite, uncontrollable, so very huge and intense, but in the end, it would have an end—her death.

She kept wondering what they were waiting for. Lying there, perhaps the waiting was the worst, to be condemned. She envisioned joining her parents in heaven. She longed for death over this extreme mental torture.

Then she smelled smoke.

Josef.

Her heart leapt a bit, though she told herself to stay calm. But she *knew* him, and he would move heaven and earth to reach her. Her clever, clever love was using kerosene and homemade explosives to smoke them out.

Vampires scurried from the chamber, their

squeals becoming more high-pitched. Ladislav ran from the room, and Elizabeth tried to get David to talk to her.

"David," she whispered. "David, please try to wake."

He only managed a confused groan, though his eyelids fluttered open.

Elizabeth heard the echoes of the vampires' screeching bounce into the cavernous room. She had absolutely no sense of direction.

A small horde of vampires returned. They were clearly agitated, pacing, hissing. They leaned over the slab, snarling. She shut her eyes, but her ears couldn't escape their noises, and she felt their frigid breath on her body. One licked her collarbone, near her neck, his tongue meaty and slimy.

The room smelled strangely of ammonia mixed with smoke, and the ever-present copper of blood. The scent of smoke grew stronger, sending the vampires into a panic. They cowered in the recesses of the chamber. Elizabeth saw that the ceiling was damp and dripped condensation.

The vampires' whispers bounced her way. They

spoke Slovak and Czech, occasionally English, and she was certain the words were vows of death and pain. The way the room echoed reminded her of a trip she and David and their father once took to Howe Caverns in upstate New York. At one point during the tour, they were in a section of the cavern that echoed the slightest whisper. She and David had delighted at speaking nearly silent words and finding the other one could hear it. But this was simply unnerving.

She lay there, arms growing numb, teeth chattering, for what seemed like an hour. The stone beneath her caused her back to ache as she waited, splayed there like an invitation to be killed in cold blood.

Cold blood. Actually, her blood would run warm until death, she mused. She wished to gaze on Josef's face one last time.

Suddenly, the vampires began squealing, baring their fangs. In strode Ladislav…with Josef.

Josef barely looked her in the eyes. What was wrong? She dared not speak his name. She held her breath. Was he a prisoner?

Ladislav approached with his son.

"The time has come, my family," he said, his voice accented, continental, charming.

Josef looked at Lad as he spoke, but still refused to look at her. Elizabeth's gut began churning even more. Had they gotten to his mind? She thought of David, how hopeless he had seemed in his cell, condemned to pitch darkness, losing his mind. What had they done to Josef, to her Josef? He gazed *admiringly* at his father.

Lad walked over to her. "I must congratulate you."

Elizabeth gazed up at him, confused and terrified. "Yes," Lad said. "It was all so perfect. You and your brother. I couldn't have choreographed it better myself."

What was he talking about? She glanced at David, and then at Josef, still not comprehending.

"Your twin comes to Prague, then when he falls ill because of some naughty little vampires, who rifle through his wallet and figure out he has a sister. He, of course, contacts her."

Lad wandered throughout the room, his boot heels clicking on the stone, his posture proud and erect. "His beautiful other half arrives. His *twin*. I have known all along the power of twins. And, I knew you'd go to the Hawthorn Inn. Everyone who passes along the mountain road is drawn to its heavy wooden doors, gargoyles gazing down."

He whirled around and poked David with the point of his leather boot. "Of course, at this point, I decided not to turn your brother. Instead, I bet on the fact that you were seers, and I was proved correct."

He cackled. "I never tire of being correct…. And your brother was worth more to me as a conduit to you. And my son."

Elizabeth glanced at Josef, who still did not acknowledge her.

"Yes, I decided your pathetic brother could be useful. He offered me a glimpse of you…but *better yet,* each time you wanted to vomit at the sight of your visions, each time you recoiled in horror, I was drawing you to this place. And with you would come…Josef."

Elizabeth's face registered confusion. Ladislav sounded like a madman. What on earth was he talking about?

"You, a damsel in distress, would bring him here.

Your pathetic attachment to your twin would mean you would ignore the dangers to yourself and my son to come here. Ironic, really. You claim to love my son, yet you were only too willing to accept his help, to risk his life, to have him die here along with you, for the sake of your brother who's been a burden to you all your life, just like your father before him."

Elizabeth shook her head. "That's not true!"

Lad bent over and slapped her across the face. "Silence or I'll kill you right now."

Elizabeth looked up at Josef. He didn't even react, didn't flinch. She felt a crushing sensation in her chest. "Do it," she said.

But instead Lad just laughed, dismissed her spark. "I knew Josef would come with you. I knew he would be curious about me."

Curious, Elizabeth thought. Josef's intentions were murderous. But now he stood next to his biological father. She wished she could talk to him alone, get him to look into her eyes, to remember their connection. Something was deeply wrong. She was his soul mate. Dhampir to seer.

Maybe that was it. He told her—right when they

first met—about his dark half, his demon half. The half that came from Lad. Maybe this bond she had with him, to his mortal side, wasn't as powerful as she thought—or at least not as powerful as the blood bond. Perhaps the beast within him was stronger than they both thought. Even thinking these thoughts made her feel disloyal. She wanted to die. Right then and there.

"I see your mind working, Elizabeth," Lad said. "The brilliant professor. Rhodes scholar?" His voice was laden with sarcasm. "I knew he would want to kill me. I've seen him hunting on the mountains. I knew about his hawthorn arrows. I'd seen the way he killed others. But, for murder or curiosity, I knew he would come here, and then my brilliant, utterly genius plan would finally come to fruition."

"What plan is that?" she managed to ask.

"My son will take his rightful place beside me. And he will turn you, and you will become his blood bride."

Chapter 23

Elizabeth felt the slab beneath her shake, as if there were an earthquake. When she looked around and saw no one else had moved or lost their balance, she realized the shock was not seismographic. It was emotional. Psychological. Spiritual. Everything she had come to believe was all wrong.

Josef had thought his father wanted to kill her and David because they were twin seers. He thought Ladislav might have wanted to mate with her. But she and Josef were as wrong as two people could be.

Ladislav had used the bond between twins. Used it to bring his son to the castle. Used it to lure them there.

She was trapped.

Ladislav continued. "I explained to my son that our people, the Gypsies, have been cursed by society, by humans, since the dawn of our existence. The human world turned a blind eye as we were marginalized. Imprisoned. Violated. Our belongings stolen, our women and children abused."

Josef looked at his father and nodded proudly. Elizabeth felt acid rising in her throat. This could not be happening.

"I was born at a time of a purge in Bohemia, before this area was the Czech Republic. The Gypsies were the lowest form of human life to the people here. My mother was beaten by an angry mob, my father murdered like a cornered animal, his body tossed in the Labe river. I vowed to become powerful. To avenge them. I apprenticed myself to another vampire and eventually became the leader you see before you. Power was the way to immortality. Anything less than ruthless power meant you could be ground up like dog meat. And then, the

Nazis." Ladislav shook his head. "The entire globe turned its eyes, shielded them from the truth. The ash that rose above Auschwitz was human—Jew, and Gypsy. The Gypsy race was virtually exterminated."

Lad bent down. "And now, seer, you will use that gift. You will *see* what happened. What the world turned a blind eye to.

With both hands, he gripped her face, and then he placed a palm on each eyelid, shutting her eyes and forcing her within.

Elizabeth was there.

"Please," a woman with dark black hair and beautiful green eyes—feline, beneath a perfectly arched brow bone—begged the guard. "Please let my child live. I will do *anything*." Her voice was laden with meaning. She would give the only thing she had to give.

The Nazi guard sneered at her. "Of course you will, you cur. Not because you have anything worth the life of your child. Her life is worth nothing anyway." He spat on the child's face. The little girl, a beautiful replica of her mother, wore the most tattered of clothes, a coat with so many patches it had ceased to be a coat and was more of a loose rag. "You will do anything I please because I say so."

The mother trembled. "Yes, sir." She cast her eyes downward.

"Get down on your knees like the dog you are!" he shouted.

The woman sank to the floor, head bowed, tears freely falling. The Nazi officer undid his shiny black belt, and unzipped his pants. He thrust his penis at her face. "Do it."

And there, shame registering on her face, the woman obeyed, performing this act like a prostitue or worse, in front of the child, who looked down.

"Watch!" he yelled at the girl, perhaps twelve, gangly, beyond that, emaciated. She watched.

And then the woman gagged. She started choking, unable to do as he asked through tears and shame and pain. She vomited.

The German looked with horror down at his penis, and then his boots and the floor. He roared, pulling away from the woman in horror. He grabbed a handkerchief from his coat, hung on a wooden peg, and wiped his member, putting it back inside his pants, and zipping up. He grabbed the woman by the hair and froced her face down into the vomit on the floor.

"See that? See that, you whore?"

"I'm so sorry. I'm so, so sorry," she pleaded, tears mixing with vomit and mucus down her face. "Please, sir. Please."

He kicked her with his heavy black boot in the stomach. Vomit now mixed with blood. Her daughter shrieked, and he slapped her full force on the face. "Shut up, Gypsy slime!"

He kicked the mother again. And again. And again. She lay on the floor, moaning in pain. He kicked her face, his boot loosening her teeth. One of her teeth flew across the wooden floor of the office.

The girl tried to cry silently, but occasionally a sob fell out. With each noise she made, he slapped her then kicked her mother harder. Blood was everywhere. But the mother was still alive.

Then he bent over and he lifted the mother's head. "Hear this, whore," he said. "I am going to rape your cur daughter now. And then I will shoot her in the head. Your efforts were useless—like the whole of your people."

Ladislav looked around the cavern. Smoke was starting to permeate, but he could still lock eyes with her.

Elizabeth couldn't help sobbing. The vision was the worst she had ever experienced. So much pain, so much degradation.

"I'm so sorry, Lad, so sorry for your people. But I am not them."

Ladislav looked around the cavern. Smoke was starting to permeate, but he could still lock eyes with her.

"The world stood silent. Jews, Gypsies, homosexuals—they didn't care until they were forced to care. Until the bombs dropped on Pearl Harbor. Before that…the world stood idly by. But my family… Gypsies…we will never be victims again! I could have killed my son. When I found him, at the foot of his mother's bed, I could have. I offered her salvation from death, from pain. I offered to turn her. I offered her to never feel pain or risk victimhood again. She refused. But her eyes betrayed her child's hiding spot."

Elizabeth watched Josef for a sign of emotion, of pain. But there was none. Not even as Lad talked of that evil night.

"I let him be. Because I knew…as a dhampir, he could turn against me, but if in time he could understand the amazing gift of immortality, strength, spontaneous healing, free from illness…and most importantly—" and at this Lad looked directly at his son "—*freedom from pain…* Then I knew he would take his place at my side."

Lad came over to Elizabeth and looked down on her. "Freedom from pain. You've seen his pain, haven't you?"

She swallowed hard and nodded.

"Let me guess," he mocked her. "You'd do anything to take his pain away?"

She nodded again.

"The irony is that *I* can take it away. His father. *Me*. Immortality will instantly cure him, instantly free him from the shackles. But only I can give him that gift. He's wanted to *die* from his pain. But I can offer him eternal life. Pain-free."

Ladislav knelt down and whispered. "Are you

willing to accept the gift of eternal life with him? He will be pain-free. Think of it."

She turned her head.

Anything but that. Doomed to a soulless existence, scurrying beneath the earth like a rat, gnawing on flesh. That wasn't existence. It was its own pain, forever.

"My son, come."

Josef stood over her.

"What have you to say to your blood bride?"

Josef sneered. "I can only imagine how soon it would have been before she tired of an invalid. Tired of caring for a cripple."

Elizabeth didn't want to cry. She knew this wasn't *her* Josef. Ladislav had obviously gotten to him somehow, the way he had gotten to David. Perhaps their father-son bond meant Lad had greater control over Josef than either she or Josef could have imagined. But much as she didn't want to cry, the sobs continued to emerge from her gut and tears rolled down her cheeks, and she saw them splash the stone slab.

Lad seemed delighted. "We will have a ceremony. My son will take you as his blood bride."

She shook her head feverishly from side to side.

"Josef, please," she begged. "Just kill me. Please. Like the Mother Superior when she wrote Father Petrochka. She begged him, if he found her turned, to kill her, not to allow her to be one of them. *Please,* Josef, let me go to my parents, to your mother. Don't…turn…me."

The last three words she whispered as her throat constricted so tightly from crying that she could barely utter the words.

She thought she saw a flash of pity in his eyes, but then he looked up at Ladislav, and all she saw was cold, reptilian murder.

"My family," Lad shouted, "we invigorate our bloodline tonight."

Josef stood next to his father. Elizabeth was amazed at how much they looked alike. Because Lad did not age, they could have been brothers, not father and son.

"Tonight, you take a bride. You cross over to death together—and then will be reborn, perfect and immortal. We, as a family, will be unstoppable. We will be powerful. We will reign together, bound by our blood."

Josef knelt at her side. He took the dagger in his

hand. Elizabeth wanted to shut her eyes, but then a part of her felt angry—terrified, but furious. She would *not* shut her eyes. She would make him see her, see *into* her heart.

Josef covered her body with his own. He had his hand on one side of her neck.

"That's it, Josef, drink. Turn her," Lad urged.

Josef suddenly screamed aloud, then he lowered his mouth to her neck. Elizabeth saw the dagger there by her neck. She waited for the pain, but didn't feel any. Her adrenaline was protecting her from the worst of this nightmare.

Josef continued to cover her body with his. Then he lifted his face.

Elizabeth screamed. Blood trailed down from his mouth and covered her neck and chest.

He was the blood son, and she was certain he had just made her his bride.

Chapter 24

"Shut her up!" Ladislav shouted.

Elizabeth continued shrieking. She was covered in blood, warm and sticky and terrifying. Was she dying? She felt no pain, though Josef was right there, covering her. What the hell was going on?

And then in one swift movement, Josef rolled from the slab, dagger in hand, stood to his full height, spun and stabbed Ladislav in the chest. Elizabeth heard a sickening moist sound, then a roar from Ladislav.

"Bastard!" Lad howled. "You could have had immortality!"

Elizabeth watched in horror. They looked so alike, it was like watching Josef kill his own twin. He twisted upward with what looked like all his strength, muscles straining, until, Elizabeth realized, he had penetrated Lad's heart.

Elizabeth was still sobbing in panic. She watched as Ladislav screamed one final, furious time, like a wolf's howl and a hawk's screech. It penetrated Elizabeth to the core of her being. It was inhuman, unnatural.

Josef twisted the knife, his face inches from Lad's. "And that is for my mother."

Lad's eyes changed from silver to pools of red. The other vampires were now hissing uncontrollably. Ladislav was dying before their eyes, aging and shriveling until he was just ash.

Josef waved his dagger at the other undead. "Get back before you meet the same demise." They retreated slightly into the shadows, cowering, but their noises were still unnerving. Elizabeth felt waves of cold passing over her, shivering in terror, unsure of what had just happened.

Josef knelt by her side and kissed her forehead. "Lad is dead," he said as he used the dagger to slice through her bonds. He grabbed her in his arms and gently rubbed her wrists to help restore circulation.

Elizabeth winced as the blood returned to her hands.

"I'm sorry, Elizabeth. I love you. I'm *sorry* I scared you. He had to be convinced I would take you as my blood bride. I couldn't betray my real emotions with so much as a look or glance. He would have spotted my love for you. He was undead for far too long. He was too clever, too evil."

She nodded, mind still reeling, adrenaline rushing through her, heart betraying her with its pounding. She looked him in the eyes. "I'm sorry I doubted you." She stared down at her chest and arms, covered in blood. "I don't understand what you did, though."

He held up his palm, which had a fierce gash across the heel of it. "When I leaned over you, I cut myself with the dagger. I had been pumping my fist to be certain there would be a good flow of blood, then I used it as theatrics."

She exhaled and tried to calm down. "I thought I had lost you."

"Lost me? I was right there the whole time, angel."

"Your soul."

He shook his head. "Never."

The clan was now howling, making it hard for Elizabeth to think, hard for her to move. She worried that she was descending into shock, and then she would be of little use to Josef as they tried to escape.

She shook her head from side to side, trying to think more clearly. "David!"

The two of them moved over to the floor where he lay. They knelt by her twin's side. She pulled David to a sitting position. His eyelids fluttered, but he was still completely out of it.

Elizabeth stroked his cheek. "Please, David, it's Lizzie. Wake up."

Josef tried shaking him. "We'll have to drag him."

But pulling David was like dragging along a bag of wet cement. Josef tried, but couldn't move him more than a couple of feet. Unless they got David up soon, there would be little hope that they wouldn't be overcome by smoke inhalation or the rest of the clan.

Elizabeth suddenly stopped. "I'll be right back, Josef."

"Where are you going?"

"Just wait."

She raced to the corridor leading out of the room where she'd been held and put her hand down on the earthen floor, which seemed alive with beetles. She grasped a handful of loose dirt and brought it to her nose. Just as she hoped—it brought tears to her eyes. She scooped up more in her hand and raced back to Josef, who held the vampires back by waving his dagger.

Elizabeth knelt by David and held the guano directly under his nose. She looked up at Josef. "Ammonia! In the guano. Ammonia is the main ingredient in caustic smelling salts."

"Brilliant," Josef said.

David fluttered his eyelids again, then violently reacted to the ammonia, retching slightly before waking up. "Jesus Christ!" he shouted. He looked around, and Elizabeth could see he was trying to orient himself.

"It's me," she told him. "We've got to go. Escape out of here. Can you stand?"

He nodded, but clearly was weak. "What the hell was that, Lizzie?"

"Don't ask."

Elizabeth helped him to his feet, and the three of them—albeit David shakily—left the sacrifice room and made their way into a long, smoke-filled corridor. Down the tunnel, they could hear vampire shrieks and the sound of rats.

"Which direction?" she asked Josef. She felt like she would die from lack of air. The walls were close, the tunnel smokey.

"Follow me. Stay close."

Elizabeth and David hurried behind Josef, ducking bats in the hot confines.

Josef took a sharp right. Ahead of them was another tunnel, but at the end of it stood a ladder.

"I think that will take us up into the castle proper. Come on."

They hurried down the corridor to the ladder.

Looking over her shoulder, Elizabeth could see that a dozen clan members had the same idea for getting out of the labyrinth.

"Josef, they're coming!"

He scrambled up the ladder, with Elizabeth next and then David. They emerged into a castle room. Elizabeth looked around. Clearly, at one time, it had been a well-appointed castle, but now it was a reminder of the decadent evil that resided there.

On one wall a mural was painted of an S&M scene worthy of the confines of hell, a scene out of de Sade himself.

"Get me those books!" Josef said. "Hurry."

Grabbing volumes of dusty editions from the shelves, David and Elizabeth brought them to Josef. He lit several on fire, creating a blaze near the trapdoor. He began dropping them down as fast as possible.

"We need a bigger blaze," Josef said.

David kept bringing books, while Elizabeth combed the room for something to ignite. She felt along the walls with her hands. A moon was out, but the light filtering in through the narrow slits of windows was gray and eerie at best. Finally, she stumbled on a kerosene lamp.

"Found something," she shouted. She brought it to Josef. He had pulled the ladder up completely, and they heard the bleating screams of vampires panicking.

Josef took the lamp from her. "You two, stand back!" He hurled the lamp down the hole, and the flames leapt up and they heard a roar of crackling fire. The heat grew very intense.

"Let's please get out of this place," Elizabeth pleaded.

The three of them left the room and ran down the hallway. It was covered in threadbare oriental rugs and the entire place smelled of mold.

They came to a room which had a crumbled wall. Cold night air blasted in, sending a shiver through Elizabeth. They still had the cold mountains to trek—only this time without their bows, without warm clothes, without food.

Josef walked to the wall and peered down. "This is a way out," he said. "But you're not going to like it."

Elizabeth came to his side and peered out. And

then down. It was a way out of the castle. Right out onto a cliff. Any missteps and they would plummet down a ravine to certain death.

"Afraid of heights?" Josef asked her.

She shook her head, for the first time realizing that after all she had experienced, she was quite certain she would never be afraid of anything again.

Chapter 25

Josef climbed through the hole first. Placing his back against the castle wall, he inched along the ledge. The twins followed his lead.

They moved slowly and deliberately. Anytime Josef thought about trying to move faster, his foot would displace a stone, and he could hear it bouncing down the canyon.

He regretted scaring Elizabeth in the sacrifice room. He looked at her bravely creeping along the ledge. He couldn't imagine her hours of mental torment. He couldn't begin to imagine David's experiences. Ladislav had used the twins' connection to lure him.

They had been wrong—so dead wrong. And it had almost cost them everything. He could never have taken his place with the clan. The thought filled him with revulsion—though, without being certain of where Elizabeth was in the maze of tunnels, he had to act with all the skills he could muster. He had to make Lad believe. He had to make him think his rightful spot was by his side.

When he had twisted the blade, it was for his mother. For both of them. And for his father. Because his true father was never Lad. It was a police detective who had raised him to be an honorable man.

Elizabeth was correct all along. His biological father's half, that dark half, was just a fraction of him. He couldn't be turned. He craved the light. He craved the goodness. Most of all, he craved Elizabeth.

The three of them began their descent. Josef needed to lead them to a safe spot in the mountains until daybreak. He had no intention of leaving the castle completely until he was certain the entire thing had burned and none of the clan remained.

When they reached a wider swath of cliff, Josef paused. He stretched his back, trying to ease the intense pain in his spine.

"Are you two okay?" he asked the twins.

David blew on his hands. "Nothing like temperatures of twenty degrees to clear your head."

Elizabeth rubbed her arms. "Cold but okay." She inhaled deeply. "I'll take the cold air—at least it's fresh."

Josef pointed toward a path carved into rock. "We'll take that to the plateau there, light a small fire, and make sure those beasts die. I don't want to see any of them taking to the night."

The twins nodded at him.

The trio made their way to the plateau, which was covered in moss and ice. Josef foraged for some kindling, and lit a fire. Elizabeth reached her hands out and warmed them by the flames. Her nails were caked with dirt and blood, her fingers scraped.

Josef looked at her face, illuminated by the orangey glow. Her neck and chest were flecked with blood. Her eyes had deep hollows beneath them. He couldn't wait until they were back at the inn, safe, clean, restored. At the thought of the inn, he felt a surge of worry for Zoltan and Anna. He hoped they were all right.

The three of them watched as the castle burned. Flames leapt from windows. Occasionally, they saw shadowy figures moving within, hurrying, panicking, but nothing emerged—no bats, no wolves, no vampires. No signs of life. No sign of the undead.

Over the hours that they watched, the sky went from midnight speckled with stars to a deep purple, and then to a bluish gray, until finally dawn arrived with a blush of rose.

"Breathtaking, isn't it?" David asked. "It's why I came here in the first place."

Elizabeth nodded. She jerked her head in the direction of the castle. "And that's an even more beautiful sight."

The castle was steaming, a hazy smoke rising to meet the coming day. Its walls were blackened, its structure even more wrecked than when they first saw it.

Josef nodded. He had done it. He had brought

the destruction to Lad's doorstep. "We had better get going. Maybe we'll be lucky and can hit the main road as darkness falls tonight. Without our equipment, it's going to be a cold hike. Danger of frostbite."

He stood and pulled off his sweater. "Now that we don't have the fire, Elizabeth, take this."

She accepted the sweater. "Thank you," she whispered, and pulled it over her head. Then, with one backward glance at the mountain, she pointed forward. "Let's go."

The three of them trudged along the path. It was arduous, with snow still covering the ground. Josef's toes and feet tingled with early frostbite, and his fingers stiffened until his hands were arthritic and closed.

Occasionally they stumbled upon a bird's nest. Once, they frightened off a doe and a yearling. Signs of life, sounds of life in the call of birds, added a hopeful feeling to the journey.

"Look!" David pointed. A black bear lumbered along about a hundred yards up the mountain.

Josef smiled. It was good to again see the woods as a place for nature, for coming spring and for the circle of life, and not as a haven for the clan. This was the Czech Republic. This was the land of his mother's people. It was the land of the Gypsies, of his ancestors. And it would be restored to its goodness.

They didn't break for lunch—for there was no lunch to have. Josef's stomach growled in protest. They were exerting themselves with no nourishment. They ate some snow for their thirst, but that was it.

The day passed and still they hiked on, exhausted and emotionally spent. Night in the mountains came rapidly. Josef guessed they were maybe two miles from the main road.

"I vote to keep going," Elizabeth said.

"Me, too," David added.

Josef concurred, and they tried to hasten their steps, though muscles and joints betrayed them.

Eventually, they heard the first car. "Oh, my God," Elizabeth cried out. "Civilization!"

The trio rushed toward the road. Elizabeth lifted her arms up. "Thank God!" She hugged David, and then wrapped her arms around Josef, kissing him and then stepping back to look into his eyes.

"We've got to get to the inn. Let's walk along the

road and see if we can't hitch a ride at some point," Josef said.

They walked in the direction of the inn, knowing they were still far from it. They heard the sound of an approaching vehicle and faced its headlights. Elizabeth waved her arms, but the truck didn't stop.

"Damn!" she said. But then she turned around and burst into squeals of nervous laughter.

"What's so funny?" Josef asked.

"If you saw the three of us roadside, would you pick us up?"

Josef eyed her. Blood spatter was flecked on her cheeks and her hair was matted and wildly askew. David looked like he hadn't seen a bar of soap in a month. And Josef knew that he was pale even on his good days, let alone after all they had been through.

"I guess not." He smiled.

They trudged on. Occasionally, a vehicle passed them by, but none slowed. After about an hour's walk, Josef realized they were within throwing distance of the affectionately named rust bucket.

Sure enough, they found their car, and after a couple of fits and starts, the engine actually turned over.

"Hurry," Elizabeth said. In the course of the night, they had told David all about Zoltan and Anna and the ominous smoke from that direction. They discovered that David had patches of amnesia over the course of the last month; he didn't really recall much of the trip there.

Josef pushed the old Renault as fast as it would allow—which wasn't very. He found himself mentally urging the car on. No heat came from its heater, and he felt like they would never stop shivering.

After two hours, in the middle of the night, they reached the turnoff for the inn. Already they could see the woods were charred and ash, a cedar graveyard. Trunks rose up like blackened sentries, letting them know death was near.

"Oh no," Elizabeth said, her voice small and broken.

Steeling himself, Josef took the turn. He owed them so much. He would find their bodies and bury them.

Chapter 26

Heartsick, Elizabeth didn't even try to fight the tears streaming down her face.

"Zoltan…Anna…" she whispered, but the words came out like a choked-off sob.

David leaned over from the backseat and patted her shoulder. Josef took her hand, his face grim as he headed down the gravel drive.

It was night, and they could barely make out the inn. The stench of smoke was heavy in the air.

"Look!" Elizabeth pointed. "The glass. The stained glass."

Josef slammed on the brakes. "Son of a bitch!" he said in awe.

Sure enough, the inn was standing. They could see the outbuildings had burned to the ground, but the inn itself was still there, though its stones were blackened. And there, flickering like a candle calling them home in the darkness, was the hawthorn glass. It was illuminated by the kerosene lamps Zoltan always left lit inside.

Elizabeth leaped from the car and ran as fast as her legs would carry her to the door and pounded on it.

No one answered.

"Zoltan, Anna! It's us!" she pleaded. She banged with her fists until they were raw. She pressed the bell until Josef came and wrapped an arm around her shoulder.

"It's no use," he said.

Then, seemingly from nowhere, Mara emerged, barking and howling.

"Damn!" David said, backing up.

Elizabeth held out her hand to Mara and spoke

to her twin. "It's okay. She's Josef's. We thought we lost her."

And then, finally, they heard the lock being opened. The big door swung wide, and standing in their robes was the old couple.

"Praise you, Mary, Mother of God," Anna whispered. She rushed forward, hugging Elizabeth, then Josef, then hugging David, who laughed as he was smothered by her.

"Oh, my goodness," Anna cried. "How we've been praying. I even got old Zoltan here to say the rosary with me."

Zoltan hugged them all as well, clearing his throat a few times.

"Come, come inside. I'll make you all some of my dumplings. And stew. And red wine."

Elizabeth couldn't believe how wonderful that sounded. They all entered the inn, which didn't look too worse for the wear.

"What happened?" she asked Zoltan and Anna.

"They came," Anna said plainly. "The beasts. They lit the forest on fire and we could hear them, howling like banshees, waiting for us to come out.

But Zoltan kept saying that the inn had survived for this long, and it would withstand the flames."

Anna led them into the kitchen where a rough-hewn table stood. She began preparing food, while Zoltan poured wine.

"We prayed to the good sisters," he said. "Smoke was choking us. We soaked towels and bedspreads in water and shoved them under the cracks in the door, but all around us the windows glowed with the orange fire."

Elizabeth gratefully sipped her wine. "And? What happened?"

"A miracle," Anna said. "The wind shifted and started the flames going towards those evil creatures, not toward the inn. By morning, the flames had nearly burned out around us, though they still were burning on the mountainside."

"And then Mara came back. She lay across the doorstep. She protected us."

"Thank God," Elizabeth said. "Thank God."

"And you? What happened?" Anna asked.

As best they could, over kolaches for dessert, they told them all that had happened.

"How did the cottage fare?" Josef asked.

"The flames took their turn before they reached it, or I'm afraid the hawthorn would have turned your cottage into kindling."

After they had drunk more wine, all of them were sleepy. David was shown to a room and a shower he said he had *dreamed* of, and Elizabeth and Josef bade them all good night and walked to the cottage.

When they parted the hawthorn and opened the door, Elizabeth felt a release, as if all her life she had never been safe, not really. Not from her father's insanity, not from their itinerant existence. Not until she came here.

Josef made a fire in the hearth and one in the wood stove. He heated water to a boil and filled the clawfoot tub in the bathroom with the lukewarm tap water, but also some pots of boiling water. Steam rose from the water. He lit a candle and showed Elizabeth to the bathroom.

"Heavenly," she murmured. She stripped out of her clothes and climbed into the tub. "Coming in?" she asked him.

He smiled and climbed in, facing her. "I don't believe hot water has ever felt so good to a man," he said.

They soaked until the water began turning cold, shampooed their hair, and climbed out. He toweled her off, then pulled her into his arms, chest to chest.

"I have to know, did you fear me, in that room? In that cavern?"

She thought carefully about her response. "No. I didn't fear you. I feared the way Ladislav was able to control minds. I feared what I saw as a seer. He shared a vision with me. I will never understand his evil, but I at least saw the tragedy behind his hatred. I feared what Lad did to David, and I feared he could somehow control you. But you, *my* Josef, no. I didn't fear. Not you."

He kissed her, and she felt the connection as strong as ever. "I would never hurt you. I'd die first," he swore to her.

She nodded. He kissed her neck and touched her shoulders, then slid his hands down. Finally, he lifted her in his arms and brought her to their bed.

"Lad thought immortality was through blood. But *this* is forever."

She took his face in her hands. "Forever," she whispered.

Epilogue

"Darling?" Elizabeth called out. "They're going to be here any minute!"

Josef rushed into the living room, arms laden with foil-wrapped Christmas presents, tied with velvet bows, which he put under the tree. Their first Christmas tree together was a huge Douglas fir, shining with white lights and Victorian-themed ornaments.

Elizabeth smiled. He looked so well, so healthy. They had returned to the United States together with David. She resumed teaching at her old post, and

Josef had concentrated on his health. Good food, rest, none of the relentless hunting, and most importantly, she was convinced, a peace of mind, had done wonders for his pain.

David had resumed writing with a fury. She occasionally saw a shadow cross his face. The memories haunted him when he was tired, but he had decided to move to Charlottesville and found an apartment near her. He now was close to finishing his novel, an epic about war between good and evil.

They had wanted Zoltan and Anna to come to the wedding that summer, but Zoltan had fought a bout of bronchitis and the doctors told him no trips across the Atlantic. They had married near Monticello, on a mountaintop, speaking vows of fidelity and trust.

Elizabeth stared down at the gold and sapphire ring on her left hand. Wrapped in the greatest nightmare of her life had been her greatest gift. She looked out the window. The Blue Ridge invoked for her a peace. A soft virgin snow had fallen, the fire in the fireplace was crackling, and the scent of hawthorn—they had planted some that summer—wafted through the air.

They didn't fool themselves. They were out there.

Other clans, other vampires. But Ladislav was gone. They knew someday they might have new battles, but for now it was a time of rest, a time of peace, a time of healing.

"They're here!" Josef said. She smiled at the little boy quality in his voice.

She stood up. David had picked up Zoltan and Anna at the Richmond airport. Two whole weeks of holiday in America. Elizabeth couldn't wait to surprise them.

Josef swung the front door open wide. Anna exclaimed, "How beautiful. The pictures don't do your home justice, you two."

Elizabeth looked around her home. It was filled with books and photos and memories and now…

She stepped out from behind her very tall and beloved husband.

"Is that?" Anna asked.

Elizabeth nodded as Zoltan and Anna rushed to her and patted her burgeoning belly.

"You two!" Anna wagged her finger. "Not telling your Anna! Shame on you."

"So you see, Anna," Elizabeth said. "You'll have to return in spring to see the baby."

Josef laughed and wrapped an arm around her, his wife. Elizabeth looked up at him and imagined his mother. She imagined her alive, in the good pictures he had. Elizabeth liked to touch Josef's curls as he slept, and she knew, in the way a woman's heart knows, that his mother must have done the same.

She smiled. And then she walked over to the window. The special window. She had a craftsman from Charlottesville make it. A stained glass window of a hawthorn tree.

It would keep them safe. It would remind them of peace. It would remind them, Elizabeth realized, of family.

She turned and looked at them all, then felt the baby kick. It was a boy. And she knew he would be as strong and beautiful and gentle and fierce as his father.

Romantic
SUSPENSE

Excitement, danger and passion guaranteed!

Same great authors and riveting editorial
you've come to know and love
from Silhouette Intimate Moments.

> *New York Times*
> bestselling author
> Beverly Barton
> is back with the
> latest installment
> in her popular
> miniseries,
> The Protectors.
> HIS ONLY
> OBSESSION
> is available
> next month from
> Silhouette®
> Romantic Suspense

Look for it wherever you buy books!

This February…

Catch NASCAR Superstar **Carl Edwards** *in*

SPEED DATING!

Kendall assesses risk for a living—
so she's the last person you'd
expect to see on the arm of a
race-car driver who thrives on the
unpredictable. But when a bizarre
turn of events—and NASCAR
hotshot Dylan Hargreave—inspire
her to trade in her ever-so-structured
existence for "life in the fast lane"
she starts to feel she might be
on to something!

Collect all 4 debut novels in the Harlequin NASCAR series.

SPEED DATING
by *USA TODAY* bestselling author
Nancy Warren

THUNDERSTRUCK
by Roxanne St. Claire

HEARTS UNDER CAUTION
by Gina Wilkins

DANGER ZONE
by Debra Webb

On sale
February
2007

Millionaire of the Month

Bound by the terms of a will,
six wealthy bachelors discover
the ultimate inheritance.

USA TODAY bestselling author
MAUREEN CHILD

Millionaire of the Month: Nathan Barrister
Source of Fortune: Hotel empire
Dominant Personality Trait: Gets what he wants

THIRTY DAY AFFAIR
SD #1785 Available in March

When Nathan Barrister arrives at the Lake Tahoe
lodge, all he can think about is how soon he can
leave. His one-month commitment feels like solitary
confinement—until a snowstorm traps him with lovely
Keira Sanders. Suddenly a thirty-day affair sounds like
just the thing to pass the time…

In April,
#1791 HIS FORBIDDEN FIANCÉE, Christie Ridgway

In May,
#1797 BOUND BY THE BABY, Susan Crosby